THREE REASONS TO LOVE

The Summerhill Series Book 3

Printed in the USA.

Cover Design and Interior Format

© THE KILLION GROUP INC.

THREE REASONS TO LOVE

THE SUMMERHILL SERIES
BOOK THREE

KEIRA MONTCLAIR

To my children.
Thank you both for being such inspirations for me,
I'm so proud of you and I love you.
To my son,
Thanks for being my inspiration for Tristan
in one very particular way.

ACKNOWLEDGEMENTS

A huge thank you to Captain Ron Poness, Jr. of the Gates Fire District for your assistance in my research of firefighting and everything it entails.

To all firefighters everywhere, thank you for the job that you do!

CHAPTER ONE

SOMEONE WANTED HER DEAD, AND they'd gone to great lengths to complete their mission. Smoke collected in her lungs, the tendrils reaching into her alveoli, choking her ability to take in oxygen, her ability to breathe, her ability to *live*.

Lauren Grant could feel the life force slipping out of her as she lay on the floor of her rented house, so close to the campus of Summerhill College, so close to help. Choking on thick smoke, she couldn't help but wonder if anyone would find her this late at night.

The fire had started in the front room of the house at around midnight. She'd gone upstairs to wash up after staying up late to work on an assignment for her Medieval Scottish History class. A loud voice shouted something outside the front windows, so she rushed into the hall, only to hear a man shout something like, "You bitch. We'll take care of you."

There was the sound of breaking glass, followed by a small explosion that shook the front of the building. The whole house filled with smoke in a matter of moments, the fire spreading with a shocking speed, basically barricading her inside. She grabbed a towel from the bathroom, crawled down the stairs, and turned the corner to try to make it out the back door, but her legs collapsed underneath her in the entrance to the kitchen.

Now she lay on the floor, covering her mouth and nose with the towel, but she feared her efforts were futile. She was not the doctor her stepfather and brother were, but she knew the dangers of smoke inhalation.

Sirens could now be heard over the crackling of the flames. Would they be able to find her in time? Male and female voices shouted at her from the front of the house, and she tried to scream, but to no avail.

"Help me." Her voice was so low and broken, no one would hear her. The voices carried to the back of the building, allowing her to make out part of their conversation.

"Is anyone inside? Who lives here?"

"Single woman. Doesn't seem like anyone's home."

Probably the firefighters talking, but she could only speculate. If she could just manage to yell or shout, but she had no energy left… She'd lost the ability to take a deep breath and, really, to be forceful about anything.

Another voice reached her, a male. "But could she be trapped inside?"

"Possibly."

"Help me, please." Her voice came out a bit louder this time, but still not loud enough. She could feel the heat from the fire. The curtains had turned to fireballs. It was only a matter of time before…

The sound of breaking glass caused her to cover her head, but she had no idea which window had blown in.

"There's a car in the driveway, so I'm going to assume someone's inside. I'm going in."

The sound of an axe splintering wood came from the back door of the house. "Anyone here? Yell out so I know where you are."

Coughing and sputtering, she summoned the energy for one last yell. Her voice came out in a screech, but she hoped it was loud enough. "Here! I'm over here." The searing heat from the flames was unbearable. She was about to be roasted alive.

She dropped her face into her hands, praying God would take her quickly.

Nathan Patterson made sure he had all the necessary gear on that he needed to go inside, including the required self-contained breathing apparatus. They'd arrived to find a working house fire, the entire building engulfed by flames. The front was much, much worse, which indicated the source of the fire could have been some sort of explosive thrown through a front window or the door as one witness's report had suggested.

After he and his partner axed down enough of the back door to climb into the house with all their gear on, Nathan yelled into the interior again. He dreaded going into the searing heat, but he had to see if anyone was inside. Intuition told him the woman might be trapped. He hoped they had a minute or two to knock the fire down and search the first floor before the second floor collapsed.

There was no response. Aiming the hose at the base of the fire, they started to move into the kitchen. He hated this part. The adrenaline took over, as it always did, but the same training that empowered him to put the adrenaline to good use also allowed him to think while he stood in the middle of all that blistering heat.

He knew exactly how a hot dog felt on a grill.

Stepping over broken glass and splintered wood, he yelled again, and this time he thought he heard a woman's voice.

"Do you see anything, Nate?" his partner yelled.

Yep, he did. The body of a woman lay just outside the kitchen. She'd pressed a towel in front of her face to help her breathe, but it had fallen away. Shit, he hoped he wasn't too late.

"Tell the EMTs to be ready for one. You're going to have to handle the hose alone." He stepped deeper into the house, and another firefighter came in behind him to help with the hose.

He bent down to get his hands underneath her, then scooped her into his arms, thanking God he'd pushed himself to build up his biceps. Lifting a dead weight was a challenge with all his heavy equipment on.

He followed the same path back out of the building, the thunder of collapsing walls trailing behind him. Just in time. Once outside, he carried her to the ambulance parked a short distance from the flames of the working fire.

"Is she alert?" asked his brother Sam, also a firefighter and an EMT.

"No, but I can see her breathing. Shallow, maybe eight to ten breaths per minute." He carried her to the back of the ambulance, setting her on the waiting gurney. The guys were prepared, and they hooked her up to oxygen right away and got her attached to a monitor. They needed to check her vital signs, see if she was getting enough oxygen.

One of the other firefighters said, "Isn't that Lauren Grant? Ryan

Ramsay's stepsister?"

Nate glanced at her. "I don't know. Never met her."

Other firefighters from another company arrived, covering the area. Nate turned around to head back to the fire, but something stopped him. He hadn't even looked at her face yet. He'd been told many times he needed to embrace the human aspect of being a firefighter, not just the battles they faced. Every year in his evaluation, he'd earned excellent marks except for the way he treated people—one supervisor had even said he treated them as if they were stuffed dolls.

How could he explain that it was his survival tactic? That he couldn't deal with the parts of the job that made it personal because of how it made him feel...and what it made him remember.

But he wanted to make captain someday. To do that, he'd been warned that he needed to learn compassion, something he'd been told again and again.

It was time to fix things. He would make himself look at this victim, if only to internalize what was at stake.

His partner yelled out, "Take a break, we don't need you right now. Captain just sent another group in. We're knocking the fire down."

Nate removed his breathing apparatus to stare at the woman in front of him. She hadn't moved yet, but Sam gave him a strange look as he checked her over. Nate moved to the side of the gurney, bending down to take a look at her. Without quite knowing why, he reached down and brushed his thumb across her cheek next to the mask, swiping at the soot there.

His brother said, "You know her?" He looked understandably puzzled—this was something Nate had never done before.

Nate shook his head. The woman's long blonde hair was completely disheveled around her face, but something about her caught his attention...even haunted him. He couldn't explain why. A few minutes later, he moved over to the truck and took off his helmet and jacket. He wasn't going back into the house, and he was far enough away not to worry about an explosion. Something about the woman niggled at him, wouldn't let go.

His brother yelled, "Go over to the second truck and get some oxygen. Looks like you could use some."

Was he right? Was that why his thinking was so odd? He took a deep breath and headed back to the truck where the victim lay on the gurney, drawn there inexplicably. "Come here," Sam said. "I'm hooking you up to a tank. You can't even follow instructions."

His brother put a mask on him and he took a few deep breaths, doing his best to expand his lungs. He sat on the back of the truck, where he had a perfect view of the victim.

Her eyes fluttered, so he leaned closer.

"What is it?" Sam asked.

"Nothing. I think she's going to open her eyes. I wonder what color they are?"

He didn't need to look at his brother's face to imagine his shocked expression. Nate Patterson didn't like to look patients in the eye, something his brother knew better than anyone. But this one was different...*she* was different.

He leaned closer, shoving the mask up on the top of his head.

"Nate, put it back on."

Shit, she was beautiful. He was taking a slow perusal of her features when her eyes suddenly opened.

Blue. Her eyes were blue. Before he could say or do anything, she threw a wild punch at his face, missing him.

"Leave me alone," she said, her voice scratchy.

He could read the fear in her gaze, something he hated. "It's all right. I'm a firefighter. I pulled you out. What's your name?" He watched her blue eyes soften as the fear dissipated.

"Lauren Grant."

"Lauren, I won't hurt you. I promise."

"Please don't," she whispered as she reached for his hand. "I'll never survive another man hurting me."

Then and there, Nate vowed to find out who had hurt her.

When Lauren awakened, she was in a hospital room with a tube in her nose, she guessed to deliver oxygen. Her hand automatically went to her temple to massage the pounding pain that reminded her something had gone completely awry last night.

It took a few minutes for her to clear her head, but memories dropped into place as she surveyed the room. She wasn't alone—her stepbrother Ryan, a police officer, stood beside his sister Mallory, a registered nurse, both of them whispering. They were dressed in their work uniforms. Mallory noticed her open eyes first.

"Lauren?" Mallory rushed to the side of the bed.

"Are you both working?" The pounding in her head refused to abate no matter how much she rubbed it.

"I was just finishing my shift when they brought you in after midnight. RJ is working the night shift. How do you feel?" Mallory was the only one who called Ryan RJ.

"I have a pounding headache, but I don't think I hit my head."

"No, there's no sign of a bump, no swelling or bruising. It's probably all the smoke you took in that's giving you the headache." Mallory brushed Lauren's hair back from her face. "I'll go find your nurse and get you something for it."

"Am I in the emergency room? Is that why you're here?"

Mallory replied, "Yes, we're just watching your breathing for a bit. RJ will explain while I go find your nurse."

She broke into a coughing fit, and Ryan reached for the water pitcher on the stand by the table. He filled a cup and handed it to her. "Here, Lauren. I think you'll need this close by. You took in a lot of smoke." His eyes were serious and showed more emotion than usual. "We're lucky the firefighters found you. Tell me what you remember."

Lauren took a sip of water, testing it, then two more sips before she set the cup down. "I couldn't get out the front door, so tried to make it around to the back, but my legs gave out before I reached the door. I was sure I was about to die. Who saved me? I have a vague memory, but I can't quite get the details."

"One of the firefighters. Nate Patterson, I believe."

"Do you know him?" Memories of his voice, his mannerisms stuck with her. She didn't know why, but they had.

"Yeah, he's a great guy. Lives with his two brothers—the youngest one just graduated high school."

"Good, maybe you can help me find him when I get out of here. I'd like to thank him."

The nurse came in to give her some pills, followed by Mallory. The nurse said, "Glad to see you awake. Tell me about your pain. Is it just in your head?"

"Yes. My head is pounding."

"You took in quite a bit of smoke, so I'd like to listen to your lungs and take your vital signs, if you don't mind. The doctor said it might be a good idea for you to spend the night. She thought it would be best to keep you on oxygen."

"I'm sure I'll be able to sleep. I'm exhausted." She took the pills and reached for the water. It was hard to swallow them down, but she managed it.

Mallory peeked over the nurse's shoulder while she placed a contraption on Lauren's finger. Once the woman finished checking all of Lauren's vitals, she said, "You're improving, so that's a wonderful sign. Let me know if those pills don't help. I can ask your doctor for something stronger."

Once she left, Mallory whispered, "Well?" to Ryan.

"I haven't gotten that far yet, Mal."

"What?"

Ryan cleared his throat and took a step closer. "Do you have any idea how the fire started?"

Lauren sighed as more memories spiraled back to her. "Yes. I was upstairs in the bathroom brushing my teeth when I heard a male voice outside. I walked down the hallway to look out the front window. The man shouted something, the front window broke, and then it was like a small explosion shook the whole house." That sound would never leave her, she was sure of it.

Why now?

Only one explanation came to mind. She'd been raped on campus as an undergraduate at Summerhill College, which had prompted her to start a support group for sexually abused women. She'd been supervised by her friend, Stacy, a social worker who'd obtained funding for a Center for Abused Women in a nearby city. After attending a session at the Center, Lauren had been inspired to offer similar services to the young women on her college campus. The support group, run under the wing of the Center, was the reason she still lived in Summerhill despite attending graduate school at Cornell. She didn't have the heart to step away from the women who needed her help.

Someone clearly didn't like the fact that she was empowering victims to stand up for themselves, or maybe her attacker objected to the free self-defense classes Lauren and Stacy had set up with cooperation from campus security. Either way, Lauren knew what the assailant had meant: stop your support group.

Well, Lauren was proud of her accomplishments—and of all the woman she and Stacy had helped. She wouldn't give up. Couldn't.

"Could you make out anything they said?" Ryan's gaze was intent, the serious expression he often carried.

"I...I think he said, 'You bitch, we'll take care of you.'"

Mallory did her best to hide her gasp, but a bit of it sneaked out. "Oh, Lauren. How awful." She moved over to squeeze her hand. "I'm so sorry."

Ryan persisted. "Any idea who might have done this? Have you received any threats from anyone lately?" He pulled out the pad he kept in his pocket to take notes.

Lauren thought for a moment, but then shook her head, only to grimace at the pain caused by the small movement. "I have no idea, Ryan. I mean, the Center is always busy. When I was visiting Stacy last week, I met with two women who'd been abused at the same frat here in Summerhill. The week before, two other women came to my group after having trouble with a different fraternity. But that's not unusual. The beginning of the year is always the worst. Lots of binge drinking before pledge week."

"Students from Summerhill went to Stacy's Center?"

"Yes. That's why I started my group. There's nothing here for victims of sexual crimes. Stacy welcomes them, and I do what I can to publicize it in Summerhill—and fill in for the people who don't want to make the journey."

"I can certainly picture a fraternity sending pledges or junior members to harass you," Ryan said, jotting something down. "Do you remember the names of the frats?"

Lauren gave him the information, but then said, "I can't give you all of the women's names, but I'll give you two." She spelled the names for him.

"Why not all four?" Ryan asked.

"Because two made me promise not to tell the police."

"Lauren, you know that could be hindering the investigation..."

"I know, but could you check the other two first, please?" Her hand came up to rub her forehead.

Ryan patted her other hand. "Never mind. I have enough to get started on. Get some rest, Lauren. I'll check the two frats to start, especially since it's the beginning of pledge season."

"But it's arson. Most of those guys would draw the line at committing a felony, wouldn't they?" She glanced from Mallory to

Ryan.

"Including rape? That doesn't fit with what you just told me. A guy who rapes a woman would commit arson to keep himself from going to jail." He glanced at Mallory to get her opinion. She gave a slight nod.

"Ryan, I don't know. Please, could I just rest right now?" She didn't want to think about this right now—*couldn't* think about it. Every day she dealt with her own memory of being raped five years ago. She didn't need this new assault to add to her trauma, but of course it would.

"I'm sorry, Lauren. Mallory will stay with you until you fall asleep. I'll check with you tomorrow." He kissed her cheek and left.

Ryan was sweet, but he didn't understand… Whenever she dealt with an abused woman, she relived her own horrible experience. Why did she continue to put herself through it?

Some days, it was just too painful to remember.

CHAPTER TWO

NATE HAD GONE BACK TO the fire station to change out of his clothes before he headed to the hospital to check on Lauren. Their shift had ended when they were on scene, so he was done for the next few days. He actually had a Friday and a Saturday off together, something he loved. His brother caught him when he came out of the locker room in a clean T-shirt and jeans. He headed for the door.

"Nate, you going home?" Sam hollered at him.

"No, I have somewhere I need to go first. Tell Tristan I'll see him later." Tristan was the youngest of the three brothers, currently a new freshman in college. He wouldn't care what Nate was doing, but Sam would. He'd ask questions if he knew Nate was headed to the hospital.

He jogged over to his truck and hopped in. Fifteen minutes later, he pulled into the Summerhill Memorial Hospital parking lot. When he cut the engine, he gripped the steering wheel before he got out of the vehicle. What the hell was he doing anyway?

Nate had seen many victims go to the hospital. After all, the town's firefighters went on all Emergency Medical Service calls as well. He couldn't even guess how many patients he'd taken to the Emergency Room as part of his work, shouting out the patient's condition as they rolled the person on a stretcher into a bay for care.

Truth was, he could only remember the name of one other patient he'd taken to the hospital. Well, he not only remembered Lauren's name, but he was also following up with a visit, something forbidden. He knew all the privacy laws by heart. It wasn't his right to ask about her—he should just wait for news, but sometimes you never heard…

For some reason, he had to know that she was all right.

There was something about Lauren Grant that wouldn't let him go. Maybe it was because he'd seen the fear in her eyes, or maybe it was what she'd said to him. That she would never survive another man hurting her. Who had hurt her?

Or maybe the problem was that he'd looked into her face and turned her from an average victim to something personal. Or was it because it had been a long time since he'd been involved with a woman? He and Mandy had broken up quite a while ago. It had been almost a year since she'd walked away from him. His brothers had been after him constantly to get over it, to get over *her*, but he couldn't yet. It wasn't that he missed her, although he did miss the companionship, it was what she'd said to him before walking out. She'd accused Nate of being overprotective. Of not being able to separate his job from his personal life. He would, she'd said, always see the people he loved as victims in need of saving.

Whatever. He'd decided it was a learning experience, only now he was wondering if he'd learned anything at all. As soon as he approached the automatic doors, he saw Ryan Ramsay headed toward him. He intercepted him, wanting an update on the situation. "Ryan, how's Lauren? She's your stepsister, right?"

"She'll be fine. A little shaken up. I think they may keep her just because of the smoke in her lungs, but she's a fighter. Hey, thanks for going in after her, Nate."

"My job, but you know that. Let me know if you find anything out about a possible arsonist."

"Will do. She's still in the emergency room, in the closed room at the end, but she looked like she was about to fall asleep. Probably best if you don't bother her."

"Thanks, Ryan. Just wanted to check on her condition before I head home." He fought the need to go inside as Ryan climbed into his patrol car, but in the end, he did the right thing and got into his truck.

She needed her sleep.

☾

That Thursday, Lauren trudged into her mother's house on the lake, thankful for the quiet, peaceful place and the long weekend that lay ahead. Her grad school classes had started, and she hadn't wanted to miss anything since it was so early in the semester, so she'd suffered the almost hour-long commute from this house almost all week. Fortunately, she had no Friday classes. Her rental had been totally destroyed, so she would be staying at the lake house for the imminent future. The level of exhaustion shooting through her indicated she probably should have taken the week off. Medieval history was not calling to her at the moment, though she normally loved it.

She made it into the kitchen and onto the back porch, her favorite place because she could look out over Orenda Lake, the serene blue water calming her soul like nothing else could. Her mother's voice came from behind her, startling her for just a moment.

"Oh, sweetheart," Lorraine Ramsay rushed to her side, giving her a sideways hug. "You might have overdone it. Look at the dark circles under your eyes. You need to rest."

"I know, Mom," she said, setting her books on the table so she could return her mother's hug, "but I didn't want to miss any classes. At least I have four days off now."

"I understand your dedication, but I hope you plan to relax this weekend. You need to take the time to heal. What a traumatic experience you've been through."

"I have no plans at all for the weekend," she said, lowering herself into one of the comfortable recliners on the porch. It was Labor Day weekend, the traditional last summer party on the lake. In Western New York, cool nights would take away the warmth of the lake, though many residents still boated through October.

"Well, remember, we do have our annual Labor Day party coming up on Saturday, but other than that you can relax all you like. And if it's too much for you, then you can just spend an hour with everyone before heading up to your room." She moved into the kitchen and returned with two glasses of iced tea, taking the seat next to her daughter. "Your only obligation until Tuesday is to take care of yourself so you can get back on your feet. No cooking, cleaning, or working. I want to spoil you."

"Oh, Mom. I think I'm past that. I'm quite capable of taking care of myself."

"I know, dear," she patted her hand. "But please don't deny me the pleasure of taking care of you. I have so little to do these days."

Her mother was still a beauty. Her skin was flawless and her hair was dark, shot through with scattered strands of white. While she was a little rounder than she'd been most of her life, her beauty had little to do with age or weight. Warmth and compassion shone in her blue eyes.

"You've worked hard raising six of us. You've earned the right to relax. Besides, you and Ryan are retired." Her mother had always wanted to be a doctor but had married young. She had five other children. Spencer was the eldest, then Lauren, Daniel, Chloe, and the twins, Colton and Lucas.

"I know, but everyone wants to feel useful and needed. Are you going to take that away from me?"

Lauren smiled and gave in to her mother. "No. I would love to have you pamper me this weekend. Though I'll warn you, much of my recuperation will be with my eyes closed in my bed."

"And that is exactly what you need. I just worry that grad school will be too much for you right now. It's a long drive."

"Mom, it's not a big deal if I have to commute to school. I like having something to keep my mind busy."

Lauren's father had passed away, but her mother was happily remarried to Ryan Ramsay, an anesthesiologist who had lost his wife to breast cancer. He was *also* a father of six. He and her mother had expanded this house to ensure it could sleep all twelve children if necessary. They were all grown children, so not many of them lived at home, but there were often visitors—from college, the service, or even those who were just back in the area.

She knew her mother needed her to talk about what happened. So far she'd managed to avoid her questions, claiming to be too tired or stressed to relive the attack. Perhaps this was the best time to be open with her. Sipping on her iced tea, she waited for her mother's questions. She said, "It's okay, Mom. You can ask me whatever you want. I'm ready to talk."

Her mother cleared her throat. Lauren recognized it as her mother's attempt to hold back tears. She hated to continually torture her mother this way—it made her feel even more helpless and out of control.

Her mother finally spoke. "What memories do you have of the fire? Do you recall anything about who could have done this to you?"

She leaned back in her chair, popping up the recliner's footrest and making herself comfortable. Then she told her mother exactly what she'd told Ryan and the other officers who'd questioned her—about the threat she'd heard through the front window, the breaking glass, and then the explosion.

"Lauren, I know you don't want to think about this, but I must ask…do you think it's possible it could be the man who raped you? He was never caught."

The rape had happened her sophomore year of college. He'd dragged her behind the bushes one night while she was walking home from the library. The rest she did her best to forget. She recalled little about him other than that he was white, dark haired, and had a worn a mask, the kind one would wear in the bitter cold of winter.

She was pretty sure it wasn't the voice she'd heard the night of the fire.

"Mom, you know I don't recall much, just his voice. From what I heard…I don't think it was the same guy. Ryan was on duty the night of the fire, but he'll talk to Jake and the other men on the force. I'm sure they'll come up with some suspects. Jake told me they've figured out which accelerant was used to start the fire. That could help them find the arsonist. I don't want to think about it this weekend, though. Let Ryan and Jake and the other guys do their jobs. Jake said they may even call in some experts from Rochester's force to help out."

"Honey…"

"Mom, please don't. I know what you're going to say." She could practically recite her mom's lecture on the importance of pursuing a normal life, including boyfriends and outings and things other than work and studying. She was always pushing her to go out, but the only places Lauren ever felt safe were family outings, especially with her two stepbrothers from the police force.

"I would be remiss as your mother if I did not mention this to you. My heart breaks for you because this man hurt you, and worse yet, he's still hurting you. You haven't dated any boys since the attack. There must be something you can do. Do you want to try another counselor?"

"No." How many counselors would it take? None of them could erase her memories. She'd tried hypnosis at her mother's insistence. No success. "I know you want grandchildren, but you'll have plenty of other…"

"That is not the point of this conversation and you know it." The pained expression on her mother's face forced her to look away.

She hated disappointing her mother.

Her mother continued pushing, as she always did. "This is about your happiness. I just think you'd be happier if you found someone to share your life with—a companion, a best friend. Someone who could help you get through this."

Lauren replied, "You know I'd like nothing more than that for myself. I just haven't been able to find a man who's willing to give up the sexual aspect of a relationship in favor of a platonic one." Not that she'd approached many about it. There was no point, was there? How many men were interested in a relationship without sex? She just couldn't imagine ever wanting anyone to touch her in an intimate way again after what that man had done to her.

"I will not belabor this. All I'm asking you to do is confide in someone. Let someone in. It doesn't have to be a boyfriend, or me, or even a counselor. Why not talk to Mallory? She's always been a good listener." Her mother let out a deep sigh. "I've said all I plan to say on the matter. You go ahead and rest. Please consider my advice." She stood up, patted her daughter's leg, and said, "I better go make that macaroni salad for dinner." She kissed her forehead and left the room.

Lauren closed her eyes and fell fast asleep, dreaming of a man with dark hair and gray eyes, someone she did not recognize. For once, it was a dream about a man that wasn't a nightmare.

☾

Nate got up early since Tristan had classes at Summerhill College. At least he would have a nice three-day weekend. They had plans to attend a picnic on Saturday, but that was it. The rest of the weekend was a wait and see situation—with any luck, they'd be invited to the lake by someone with a house and a boat on the waterfront.

He looked at the clock as soon as he stepped out of the shower, wondering why Tristan wasn't up yet. Shit, sometimes he hated having to play mother to Tristan. Their mom had died in a car accident and their father had bailed on them two years later, so it had been just the three of them for the last five years. Nate was the eldest, so responsibilities fell on his shoulders.

True, Sam helped support Tristan and the house their parents had left them, but it still felt like a heavy load at times. How many times had he wished he could just forget everything? Do what he wanted without worrying about other people?

No. He loved his brothers. He'd be alone otherwise. "Tristan?" He wrapped a towel around his waist and marched down the hallway in his bare feet. "Tristan," he said again, sticking his head in his brother's room, "don't you have class today?"

His brother's tawny head stuck out of the covers as he groaned, "Go away."

"Don't you have class?"

"Yeah, but I'm in college now. I don't have to go if I don't want to." He rolled over and covered his head with the blanket.

"Get your ass out of that bed and go. True, you don't have to go, but that's a great way to guarantee failure."

"Stop acting like my mother again, Nate. Get the hell out of my room." His voice was completely muffled by the blankets.

Nate strode over and yanked on the bed covers, pulling on them until Tristan almost tumbled out of bed.

Tristan sat up to keep from falling. "What the hell?"

"Get up. You may have a partial scholarship, but you won't have one for long if you keep slacking off. There's a difference between high school and college, all right. College costs money."

"All right. I'll go. Just get out." Tristan looked like hell, like he'd had too many beers last night. He and Sam had agreed to allow their brother to drink a few beers even though he was under the legal drinking age of twenty-one in New York State, but only as long as it didn't affect his classes and he never drove under the influence.

Sam came along and stuck his head in the door. "Aren't you supposed to get a group assignment today? If you don't go, you'll be stuck with all the leftover losers."

"Yeah, in one class." That got his attention. He climbed out of bed, but not before griping, "All my friends told me college is supposed to be a big party." He grabbed some clothes and headed to the shower.

Sam called out after him, "If you don't go to any of your classes, you're not going to meet any of the hot girls."

Tristan slammed the bathroom door, but at least he was getting ready.

"Thanks for talking some sense into him. What the hell has gotten into him lately?" Nate asked as he headed to the kitchen, Sam behind him.

"He's eighteen, or have you forgotten what that feels like?"

"I lost my mother at eighteen. Kind of ruined a lot of things for me. I try my best to forget that year."

Sam ran his hand through his hair. "Yeah, I know. But look at it this way—he graduated high school with good grades. Now it's time for us to ease up a bit. He's a good kid. He'll figure it out."

Nate sighed as he poured himself cup of coffee from the coffeemaker. "I know. I just can't seem to stop." He sat down at the kitchen table, pulling his phone out.

Sam said, "Mandy was right, you know."

Nate set his coffee cup down and looked up at his brother with a narrowed gaze. "Right about what?"

"You're overprotective, especially when it comes to us." Sam grabbed a bowl out of the cupboard and a box of cereal, their usual breakfast. "If you stopped trying to control us, there'd be fewer fights."

Nate slammed his coffee cup down, spilling liquid over the edges, and grabbed his phone. He walked out of the door without a word, but Sam wouldn't leave it at that.

"Where are you going?"

"Fishing. Somewhere where I can't control you. Enjoy."

"What's with the stick up your ass?" Sam asked. "I was just trying to talk."

Nate didn't answer. He just headed out to the garage and gathered his fishing gear, threw it into the back of the truck. No one would bother him at the local fishing pier, where peace and quiet ruled. It would be just him and the fish.

Maybe Mandy was right...*and* Sam. A shrink would probably tell him he was overbearing because he felt like he had no control in his life.

And they would be right.

Something else was on his mind, too. Something he didn't care to share with anyone. He couldn't stop thinking about Lauren Grant. And sometimes he'd wake up in the middle of the night with a hard-on like he hadn't had in months.

All because he'd looked at her. Now his world was spiraling out of control and he didn't like it at all.

Not one bit.

CHAPTER THREE

LAUREN STARED AT THE VOLLEYBALL game being played outside her window. It was their annual Labor Day picnic. The sun was shining and it was a lovely seventy-five degrees, but she couldn't bring herself to come down to the party yet. A knock sounded at her door, and though she almost ignored it, she said, "Come in."

Ryan's wife, Caitlyn, stood in the doorway. "Hey, Lauren. I'm sorry to bother you."

"Come on in, Cait. You have the weekend off? How nice." Caitlyn was an RN at a pediatric hospital, which required her to work every other weekend and many holidays.

"This is one of Ryan's favorite parties, so I put in for it a while ago. How are you doing?"

"I'm okay." She sat on the bed and motioned for Caitlyn to sit next to her. "I can't seem to adjust to the fact that someone tried to kill me. I guess that's what's dragging me down." That, and the trauma of her rape resurfacing. Every time she thought she had put it solidly in her past, something freshened the wound.

The powerlessness, the anger, the sick feeling from that horrible man's touch... She gazed off at her desk and her laptop, thinking about the message she had received in her school email account late last night. "Stop running the group. Leave it closed and I'll leave you alone." She'd called Ryan about it and the cops had checked it out, but they hadn't yet traced the original sender.

Was it possible her mother was right? Was the man who'd set her rental on fire the same man who'd raped her five years ago? Had he raped others? Was that why he'd destroyed her home? Or maybe her original theory had been correct, and she was being harassed by someone who'd abused—or tried to abuse—one of the women she'd helped. She feared she'd never know.

Cait reached over for her hand. "Lauren? Why don't you come downstairs? I know you're tired, but I think it would be good for you. There's someone here who would like to meet you."

"Huh? Someone wants to meet me? If it's a guy, I'm not ready..." It was much safer for her to stay alone in her room. If she went out there and talked to everyone, they might ask her about what had happened. Then the fire—and the rape—would replay in her head like horrible movies.

"It's the firefighter who saved you. His name is Nate Patterson. He's here with his two brothers. They're all playing volleyball, but he wanted to talk to you, make sure you're okay."

"Oh. That would be nice." She supposed she would have to force herself to speak with him. It was only proper to thank the man who'd saved your life. Should she tell him that a small part of her would have been okay if he hadn't saved her?

No. She needed to be stronger than that—stronger than the bad things that had happened to her. There was so much to live for. Her family was wonderful, she'd helped many other assault survivors, and she'd just uncovered a fascinating battle in her study of Scottish medieval history.

And yet she couldn't forget.

Cait wouldn't let up. "Why don't you come down and meet him?"

Lauren stood with a smile, telling a silent lie, just like she did every day. It was the only way she could manage to act "normal."

"I'd like that. Let me freshen up first." She headed into the bathroom next to her room to brush her teeth and comb her hair. Her mother was right—the dark circles under her eyes were still there. How did one get rid of those? Sleep, the one thing she couldn't seem to get because her sleep was haunted—haunted by a voice calling her "bitch."

She opened the door and nodded to Cait, who led her down the stairs and out onto the expansive lawn in front of the lake. "I'll see if I can find him."

"Okay. I'll wait in the gazebo." She made a point of walking around the groups of people chatting on their own. She wasn't up to making small talk that would inevitably lead to the fire.

Staring out over the lake, she found herself hoping Nate was nice. He was a firefighter, which meant he was likely responsible and hard-working, and he was certainly brave—all qualities she would look for in a man…were she interested in finding one. She heard Cait's voice and pivoted.

Every thought left her head. Nate Patterson was gorgeous… probably the most attractive guy she'd ever met. His dark hair was short, and he had gray eyes that reached out to her. She didn't understand that. Though she didn't remember being rescued by this man, he did look strangely familiar.

Then it hit her—Nate was the man in her dream. How was that possible? She'd never been a believer in psychics or anything otherworldly. Had her unconscious mind just retained the memory of him rescuing her?

She smiled as Cait introduced them. After giving his hand a firm shake, she said, "It's nice to meet you, Nate. I'd like to thank you for saving me at my rental. I tried to get out…" Her voice caught as a flood of emotion swept over her, and she dropped her gaze to her feet.

Cait said, "I promised Lorraine I'd help her in the kitchen, so have fun and thanks for coming, Nate."

The man was so handsome that it left her tongue tied, something that never happened to her. He had on a plain white T-shirt that stretched across his chest, showing off his musculature to anyone who was interested. His body was incredible—tanned, toned, muscular, begging to be touched… *Men this strong are dangerous*, a voice in her head whispered. *He could crush you without even trying.*

And yet, she somehow knew he wouldn't.

"Lauren, no need to thank me. It's my job, but I wanted to make sure you were all right. You had taken in a lot of smoke." He smiled, the kind of smile you saw on dental ads.

Lauren sat down because she had to. He sat close, but far enough away so they did not touch, which suited her fine. She didn't allow strange men to touch her…ever. "I'm fine. So do you like firefighting? It must be quite terrifying at times."

He laughed, and the sound seemed to shoot to her sex, to the tips of her breasts. She tried her best to stop the raw response her body had to Nate Patterson, but she couldn't. No man had affected her like this since the rape. Licking her dry lips, she couldn't help but stare at him.

"It is terrifying and exhilarating at the same time. Does that make any sense?" He ran his hand through his short hair. She could see how much he loved his work in his eyes. His smile making her want to sigh, to touch him, anything. "Jake said you're attending Cornell University. What's your major?"

"I'm hoping to obtain my Master's Degree in history. I thought I wanted to teach, but I'm so drawn to medieval history that I've changed my focus."

"Medieval history. Wow. That's different."

She gave him a look.

"No, I'm sorry," he said, lifting a hand. "I didn't mean for it to come out that way. I meant *good* different. I haven't met anyone involved in that type of pursuit." He flashed another gorgeous smile her way. "What area are you studying? Something specific or a global study?"

She was surprised he was interested enough to press for more information. Most people heard the word history and shut down completely. "I started studying England, but I feel more drawn to the Scottish Highlands, probably because there's so little documented history, especially in the 1200s, which is the time period I've been researching. When I finally find something, it's like finding a rare treasure."

He gazed into her eyes, but she had to pull back. If she didn't, she would become lost in those beautiful orbs. Much better to ignore him. There was no man alive who would choose to deal with someone like her, someone with intimacy issues. Perhaps it would be best to end this conversation.

"Again, I don't know how to thank you for saving me."

"You're welcome. Now I have to ask a favor." He made the statement with such a serious expression on his face, she had no idea what he was about to say, and she felt an urge to bail out of the situation—the way she bailed out of everything.

"Sure." She said it hesitantly, but how could she refuse the man who had saved her life?

"Promise me you won't thank me again? You've thanked me enough, and I would like to put that behind us."

She couldn't help but laugh. "All right, I agree to your request."

"Have you returned to your place? I mean, has anyone allowed you back in to see if you can salvage anything?"

He stood and took a step closer, and she had to fight her instinct to get up and move away from him. *He will not hurt you, Lauren, he will not grab you or push you...This is the man who saved your life.*

He'd asked her a question, hadn't he?

Oh! The scene of the fire. She'd thought about going back, but she hadn't yet built up the nerve. Still, she needed to see if the information in the lockbox was safe. "No. Would that be possible?" she asked. "I haven't even driven past since it happened, but my stepdad did. He said there wasn't much left to the building. But there is something I need...if it survived the fire. It was in a protective box. Who could I see about having it returned? It was supposed to withstand extreme temperatures."

"Let me make a couple of calls and see if it has been cleared by the fire marshal." He took out his phone and stepped outside the gazebo across the grass to make his phone calls.

Would going back resurface more memories?

Probably, but she needed the contents of that box. True, the information in there was backed up on her flash drive. Didn't matter. She wanted the written copy.

Taking a deep breath, she said a quick prayer for strength because she'd vowed not to allow criminals to change anything she did. She refused to give them that satisfaction.

Nate cleared his throat, bringing her back to the present moment. He stood with one leg on the first step of the gazebo, his phone back in his pocket. "It's been cleared. I'd be happy to take you over there if you'd like. Officially, you shouldn't go in without a firefighter or the fire marshal. It could be dangerous, but I know what to look for when it involves burned walls and the like. But you might want to put on dark clothes and dark sneakers. The soot could get all over you."

"Thank you. I'll go inside to change and let my mom know I'm going with you." Then she blushed. "Not that I'm required to or anything, I'm plenty old enough, but she's a little worried about me after what happened. She'd feel better knowing I left with you."

"I completely understand. I'd be happy to answer her questions while you change."

"Perfect. Why don't you come with me?"

She headed back to the house, glad he had suggested she change out of her white pants. They certainly would have been ruined by the expedition. Her mother was still in the kitchen, fussing over the meal.

"Oh, there you are, Lauren. Have you eaten?" Her mother's eyes widened, and Lauren could tell she'd just noticed Nate behind her.

"Mom, I'd like you to meet Nate Patterson, the firefighter who carried me out of the blaze. He's going to take me back to my house to see if anything is salvageable." She could tell how pleased her mother was by her statement, so she ducked away from them. "I'm just going to go change."

"Nate, I owe you so much for saving my daughter. Bless you."

Lauren ran up the stairs. She didn't want to leave Nate with her mother for too long. If she did, she might come back to find herself in an arranged marriage.

☾

Nate looked up as soon as Lauren entered the room a few moments later. Hell, but even dressed down she was beautiful. She had on a dark T-shirt, dark jeans, and dark sneakers. Perfect attire for digging through the ashes. She'd even pulled her hair into a bun on top of her head, another wise move. Her golden hair could be covered with soot in no time.

She gave her mother a kiss on her cheek and said, "We'll be back soon."

Cait, who was helping out in the kitchen, called out her name. As soon as Lauren turned around, Cait tossed her a few packets. Lauren held them out for him to see.

"Ah, wet wipes. Smart girl."

"Cait is a nurse. She thinks of everything." They headed out the door and he led her over to his truck.

Nate held the door for her and she climbed up easily—a good sign that she was recovering from the incident. She put her seat belt on and waited for him to get in. When was the last time he'd had a woman this beautiful in his truck? Seeing her in person again had made him realize—and accept—that he was interested in her. Very interested. If he had his way, he'd tug her over onto his lap and kiss her before they even backed out of the driveway.

But this time, he was determined to do things right. No one

would accuse him of being overprotective or controlling. He could tell she was as nervous as he was, so he decided to start a conversation. "You have quite a large family. How do you keep track of everyone?"

She laughed, a sweet musical sound. "It is difficult some days. Especially because we aren't all in the area."

"How many siblings?"

"I have four brothers, a sister, and six stepsiblings. We can have a huge party all by ourselves."

"And is there room for all of you at the lake house?"

"Yes, my mother squeezed in beds and trundles and all kinds of things to fit us all, although I don't remember how long it's been since we were all together. How about you? I remember Ryan and Cait telling me that you have two brothers."

"Yes, it's just the three of us. We live together in my parents' house."

"I don't mean to be nosy, but where are your parents?"

"My mother died in a car accident several years ago, and my father couldn't handle raising us alone. He left a couple of years later, but at least the house had been paid for."

"Oh, I'm so sorry to hear about your mother."

"Thanks. Here we are." He turned the engine off in front of the house, allowing her the chance to look at everything before he got out. The house was roped off because the site was still dangerous. "As you can see, the second story collapsed, but many of the first-floor walls are still standing."

She opened the door and got out, not taking her eyes off the place she used to call home. He jumped out, running over to her side to guide her. "It would probably be best if we entered the ruins from the back."

"Have they found anything to prove who did it?" She followed him down the driveway to the back of the house.

"Not that I know of, but I'll check for you the next time I go in. Has Ryan said anything?"

"Just that they have a couple of leads, but he hasn't shared them with me. He's been working with a group of detectives, even a couple from Rochester. Ryan said the chief has made the case a priority so they're all working on it. Actually, I don't want to know what's going on until they're sure."

She made her way to the back door, which was hanging on its hinges, and stepped inside. She stumbled and he caught her. "Here, hold my hand so you don't fall. We'll both prop each other up. Do you remember where you kept the lockbox?"

"Yes. It was on the top shelf of the downstairs closet near the kitchen." She pointed in the direction for him to go.

"Why don't you stay out here while I check? If it made it through, it should be easy to find." She nodded, and he moved carefully through the debris, hoping the foundation held him up. He yanked on the closet door to see if it would open, and it fell, half of the wood in the door charred beyond recognition. He shoved some broken boards around, and finally found something.

"Did you find it?" Her voice carried through to him, a little more anxious than he'd expected, making him wonder what was inside the box.

"Yeah, I think so." He came out with the black box in his hand, the lock still in place. "Is this what you're looking for?"

"Yes." Her face lit up. "Thank you. I keep some important papers in there, but there are also some things inside that are quite special to me. My father gave me a necklace the year before he died."

"I'm sure it's probably still in there, but I think it would be better for us to get outside and open it there." He helped her back outside, carrying the box for her. As if she could not wait another moment, she took the box from him and sat down on the front porch steps, still intact. After using one of Cait's wipes to clean all the soot off the box, she opened it with the key code. He could see the relief on her face as she withdrew the necklace. It was clearly very special to her. She replaced the necklace, closed the box up again, and rubbed her fingers across the metal, staring down at it.

"Are you all right, Lauren?" He didn't know quite what to do or say at this point. It had to be devastating to see your home destroyed like this. This was the part of firefighting he usually did his best to stay away from—the personal piece.

She nodded, standing up and pivoting to stare at her house. "This was all I came for." She stared up at the house. "I still can't believe it happened, but it was only a rental. Everything else inside is replaceable."

He gave her a moment to process, then placed his hand at the small of her back. "Why don't we go? Unless there's something else you wanted to see."

"No." She lifted her chin. "Thanks for bringing me here. It means a lot to me, but I have all I need from this house."

They walked back down the driveway in silence. He opened the door to his truck, but before she got in, she turned to face the house again.

"Maybe for some odd reason, this will turn out to be a blessing." She smiled and climbed into the truck.

He wondered what she meant by that.

CHAPTER FOUR

ALL THE WAY BACK TO her house, Lauren couldn't stop thinking about what she'd just seen. Her home had been destroyed. But she'd been able to retrieve the most important contents of that house thanks to Nate, and it was safe on her lap. She was beyond relieved the necklace from her dad had survived, but she *needed* the chart she'd made. It was her best hope for stopping the pattern of sexual abuse on campus. For finally putting the past behind her—something she was very ready to do.

She glanced at Nate, realizing she was probably being rude by ignoring him. "Sorry, but I'm lost in my own thoughts. It brought back many memories."

"It's all right. We don't need to talk. It was a lot to absorb."

She turned her gaze away from him, staring out the window at the lush greenery of Upstate New York. Maybe it was time for her to move away from her hometown, make a clean sweep of everything, find a place where no one would know her, or know her past. As it was, everyone was aware of her trauma since the newspaper had printed a full story about her attack and a few follow-up stories about the polices' attempt to find the criminal. Of course, they hadn't identified her by name, but everyone had known nonetheless.

When they reached her house, Nate pulled in, looking for a place to park. She pointed off to the side. "That's my car. You can park behind me. I'm not leaving."

He parked his truck but left the engine running and turned to her. "Are you all right?"

She nodded, unable to speak through the lump in her throat—something to which she'd sadly become accustomed. How she hated that she couldn't wipe the dark memories out of her mind, or put them in a strongbox to be pulled out only when absolutely necessary. Now, she had two traumatic memories that would always niggle at her, threatening to pop out at the worst of times.

"Look, Lauren, I...well, I'm guessing you may have been attacked yourself since you started that group Ryan told me about."

He waited until she gave a quick, sharp nod, which was all she could manage at the moment.

"I'm not involved with anyone at the moment, haven't been for a while, and I'm wondering if you'd consider grabbing a bite to eat with me sometime."

"I don't go out much. Only to classes and to the library." She stared at him. How she wished to say yes... How she wished she could hand her heart to him, throw her arms around his neck, and embrace a relationship with him. But something was still broken inside her, and the only words she could get out were, "I'm sorry."

"For what? You have nothing to be sorry about." He reached for her hand and ran his thumb across the back. "Do me a favor and take my phone number, just in case you need help with anything. Text me anytime."

Her gaze stayed on his hand, reveling in the gentleness of his touch even though they were callused, hard-working hands. They were powerful, yes, but her intuition told her that he would never use them against her. What could it hurt to exchange numbers with a firefighter? The man who'd saved her life?

She pulled her phone out, and they exchanged numbers. For some reason, having his number made her feel better, but it didn't change what she was—a burden. A messed-up burden.

"Nate, I'm too messed up to be any good to anyone. I'm sorry." She grabbed the metal box, climbed out of the truck, and ran. It felt like hands clawed at her, trying to hold her back and imprison her, but the logical part of her brain knew no one was following her. Tearing up the stairs, she finally reached her room and closed the door behind her, gasping for air for a few minutes until she was able to throw herself on the bed and erupt in tears.

Once her tears were mostly spent, she managed to climb off her bed and make her way to the window. A volleyball game was in play not far from beneath her window. She pulled the curtain back just a touch to see if Nate was there.

He was. He'd taken his shirt off, and she was close enough to appreciate the muscles rippling across his back each time he leaped into the air for the ball, trying his best to spike it toward the opposite team. Watching Nate play was like admiring a thing of beauty. The breeze carried his laughter up to her. What would it be like to have a guy like that to hold you, to protect you, to stand in a crowd with his hand at the small of your back, making a small claim that you were his?

It was an antiquated thought, she knew, but there was plenty of appeal to it. As a medievalist, she often wished for a brawny Highlander to protect her. A strapping Scot who would stride behind her carrying a claymore, poised to strike at anyone who dared to touch her. Or maybe an honorable English knight.

How she wished she'd had a Highlander to protect her that fateful day. How had she let a one-hour assault five years ago take over her life?

Because she was helpless to stop it. No matter how hard she tried, no matter how many counselors she saw, that memory ripped her insides out over and over again, whenever it chose to rear its ugly head.

It wouldn't be fair to foist herself on someone as noble as Nate Patterson.

She dropped the curtain and turned away from the game. Fear of being seen forced her back to her bed, but she left the window open. Listening to the playful banter and the laughter between the players was far better than listening to what was in her own head.

A few minutes later, she heard the celebration of the end of the match. Nate's team had won. The next thing she heard was Mallory begging Ryan and Jake to take her water-skiing. Then Ryan said, "Sure, Mal. Patterson, do you want to join us?"

Nate said, "Absolutely. I'll get my suit on."

Lauren did something she'd never done before. As soon as Nate disappeared, she leaned out the window and yelled, "I want to go, Ryan. Please?"

Ryan and Mallory both stared at her in shock. Her stepbrother was the first to recover. "Sure. I'll wait while you put your suit on, Lauren."

Mallory yelled to Lauren, "I'll be right up."

What had she done?

ᘓ

Nate spoke to his brothers before he headed out to his truck for his suit. He'd driven separately because he was on call, but he had hoped he'd have the entire day to himself. There was nothing he loved better than boating. After changing in the boathouse, he headed over to the speedboat and asked Ryan, "Your sisters all like to ski?" What he really wanted to ask was if Lauren liked it.

"Mallory's the best of any of us, but we all like to ski." Ryan fiddled with the equipment on the boat and set his phone in a compartment. Jake played around behind him, getting the boat ready to go out. "It's been a warm summer, so the water isn't too bad, but the cool nights are about to settle in. Might as well get out there while we still can. You ski, Nate?"

"Not much. Tried a couple of times, but I'm not great at it."

Ryan said, "Watch Mallory. She's a pro. There'll be plenty of boats on the water this weekend—lots of wakes to manage. Jake usually takes the boat out, but he's a little too wild with it."

Jake, who he knew through the department, said, "You know where you can shove that comment, Ryan." He grinned at Nate. "No sense in making it easy for anyone. It's more of a challenge the way I drive. Too bad Julia's not here yet. Otherwise I would show you how it's done."

Cait came rushing down the small hill toward the boat. "Ryan, Lauren's coming." She stopped as soon as she saw Nate. "Oh, sorry. I didn't see you there." Turning back to Ryan, she added, "Who convinced her to come?"

Ryan shrugged. "She's the one who suggested it. She overheard Mallory and me making plans. I'm glad. She needs to get out more, especially after that damn fire."

A shock of anticipation rushed through Nate. He hadn't thought he'd see her again today, not after the way she'd raced away from the truck. Glancing up at the house, he caught sight of the stunning beauty as she strolled across the grass and down toward the water's edge. She had a wrap of some kind over her bathing suit, but it didn't hide much of her long shapely legs. Nate couldn't take his eyes off her.

Mallory raced along at her stepsister's side like a hyperactive five-year-old, hooting about going skiing. Her voice carried down to the water. "Come on, Lauren. Maybe we'll get you up on skis today. It's great weather for it." He'd bet she must have been a cheerleader in high school.

Lauren shook her head. "I don't know if I'm up for *that*. You know I'm not very good at skiing."

What a contradiction she was... She carried herself with confidence, her shoulders held back, her chin lifted, and a small smile on her face, all properly prepared for anyone who looked at her. But he saw something else roiling beneath it—he saw it in the fear in her gaze, her death grip on the beach towel she carried, and her darting eyes. Her pain was hidden behind a façade that was carefully constructed and painstakingly maintained.

He'd do his best to break through that barrier of hers. Even if they couldn't make something work, he still vowed to try. He wanted to know her.

As she approached the boat, she shot him a look and then quickly glanced away, her cheeks slightly pink. Maybe she was embarrassed about what had happened earlier. Well, there was no reason for her to be, and he would do what he could to prove that to her.

Ryan said, "Let's go. Mallory, choose your skis."

Mallory was already headed to the boathouse. She was inside for less than a minute before she emerged with her life vest and skis in hand, a broad smile across her face. Ryan led them to the boat and Nate hopped in first, turning around to help Lauren board the boat. She reached for his hand and froze, pausing for just a second before placing her hand in his and stepping into the boat. A small wave rocked the vessel, and she touched his chest to balance herself—then removed her hand as quickly as if he'd burned her.

"Whoa, hang on, Lauren."

She gave him her practiced smile before she straightened and tucked into the corner of the back of the boat. There were two seats in front, one for the driver, and the back had two rows of cushioned benches facing each other. It would easily fit three on either side. Cait sat in the seat next to Ryan, so Nate sat across from Lauren to balance the weight of the boat.

Nate untied the back rope once Ryan started the motor, standing again to shove away from the dock. Mallory, who'd already donned her life jacket, sat on the end of the dock and secured the skis on her feet. "Don't get me wet, dear brother."

Jake stood not far behind her on the dock. "Don't use all of your energy now, Mallory. Come out on the boat with Julia and me later. I'll make it more of a challenge for you."

She ignored him.

"How far do you want to go?" Ryan shouted over the sound of the motor.

"Our usual trip is fine." She rolled something off her wrist and wrapped it around her dark hair, popping her long locks into a ponytail in a matter of seconds.

"Make sure you don't go too fast for Mallory," Jake shouted. "You know she's just learning."

Mallory flipped her brother off over her head.

Nate chuckled at the playful sibling behavior, then glanced up at the perfect sky, brilliant blue with a few cumulus clouds completing the pretty picture. "Beautiful day, Lauren."

She reached into her small bag and put her sunglasses on. "It is. A perfect day."

Cait jumped right into the conversation. "Do you boat much, Nate?"

"Every chance I get, though I don't own a boat. I love to fish."

"Come down any weekend," Ryan said. "There's always somebody taking the boat out, even into October."

Cait grinned. "I love the autumn leaves, just trolling through the water and enjoying the view. The lake is much quieter then." She tipped her head back to soak in the warm sun. "Still, I'm sad that summer is over. Autumn is pretty and calm, but summer is what it's all about."

Ryan positioned the boat right in front of Mallory, and Cait handed the tow rope to Nate. "You can probably throw it farther than I can. I'm terrible at it."

He took it from her and tossed the end to Mallory.

"Perfect, Nate."

Once Mallory had a solid hold on the rope, Ryan puttered the boat out until he had the full line out, then yelled, "Tell me when."

Mallory gave him a thumbs up, "Go, RJ!"

Ryan waited until she had both hands securely gripping the tow rope, then gunned the engine, making sure he gave Mallory a strong pull to keep her from toppling into the water.

Once Ryan hit his top speed, Mallory glided across the water like she'd been born on skis, her laughter making all of them smile. She moved across the wakes without a blip in her composure or balance.

Nate glanced at Lauren. "Have you tried skiing?"

She smiled. "I've tried a couple of times, but I can't manage to stay up. My legs give out."

Ryan glanced back at her as he made a slow turn of the wheel. "You want to try today, Lauren? I'll go slow, just take you around the cove. There's no wind."

"I'll think about it."

Cait said, "Mallory can sit in the water with you, help you do it."

"Maybe."

Lauren shifted her gaze to Mallory, who was now giving Ryan the thumbs-up sign again.

"Faster, Ryan," Lauren relayed.

"You asked for it, Mal." Ryan cranked the motor up and Mallory flew across the water.

Out of nowhere a speedboat moved in behind them, cutting way too close for comfort.

Ryan shouted, "Too close, asshole!" though Nate doubted they could hear him.

The boat was full of five men, holding beer cans up to Mallory, who promptly flipped them off without losing her control.

"Cait, can you tell who's out there?" Ryan asked.

She shook her head before shifting her gaze to Nate and Lauren. "Do you recognize any of them?"

"I do," Lauren said. "Local guys."

The boat headed off to the middle of the lake, so Ryan turned around and headed back toward their cottage. He pulled in close to shore, giving Mallory the perfect opening to glide in and land just in front of their dock. Then he swung the boat around and cut the engine, crawling in closer to the dock.

"Who were those dickheads?" Mallory yelled. "I thought I recognized one, but I didn't know the others."

Everyone on the boat turned toward Lauren.

Lauren said, "I recognized two of them. Dominic Miller was driving the boat and Trevor Hutton was in the back. Dom is attending Summerhill College. I'm pretty sure Trevor already graduated from Summerhill. He was a year behind me in high school, and he actually asked me to the prom. I've seen Dom in the library before. He always talks too loud. Kind of obnoxious."

Cait asked, "Did you go to the prom with Trevor?"

Lauren just shook her head. "I didn't go at all."

Nate couldn't believe she'd never gone to the prom. She should have been the queen. Of course, he hadn't gone either, but for a completely different reason.

Ryan suddenly perked up. "Do they belong to a fraternity, Lauren?"

"I'm not sure, but I think Dom does, and not one of the nice frats either."

Nate knew exactly what Ryan was thinking. He was wondering whether there was a connection between any of those guys and the person who'd started the fire at Lauren's rental.

"What do you mean by nice frats, Lauren?" Nate asked.

She shrugged. "A lot of women come to me after being attacked at frat functions, especially around pledge season. They drink too much, and the guys talk them into something stupid before they realize it."

"Like what?" Ryan asked.

"Like chugging and drinking so much that they black out or their memories turn hazy. Or taking pills that alter their consciousness. Some of them won't consider testifying because they don't want their parents to find out what they were doing. And some frats are known for that kind of thing more than others."

"Then why doesn't the school shut them down?" Cait asked. "If it's that obvious."

"That's a great question. I wish I had the answer."

Everyone looked to Ryan, who shrugged his shoulders. "We're not supposed to be on campus unless we're invited, though that could be changing soon."

Mallory said, "You need to push that rule, RJ. You, too, Jake." Then she turned to Lauren. "Anyone you suspect in particular?"

Lauren shrugged her shoulders. "I didn't get a look at the man who broke the window. I only heard a voice."

"Aren't you attending Cornell?" Nate asked out of nowhere.

"Yes, but I didn't want to close down my support group. Besides, Summerhill's library has a wonderful section on medieval history. I spend a lot of time there."

Nate asked, "Don't you do your research online?"

"Sometimes," she said. "I love the library. I know that sounds foolish, but I work really well where it's quiet."

Nate didn't need to ask her to explain that response. People didn't typically get attacked in the library—they weren't even allowed to talk under most circumstances. Lauren went because it was a safe place, though that was an assumption because he had no idea where her first attack had taken place.

When they got close enough to the dock, Mallory said, "I know Dom. He's arrogant and obnoxious, everything Lauren said. I don't know Trevor, but I think Randy Brooks was with them. I remember him from high school. The kind of guy who liked to leer at your breasts all day and then smile at you. He's a pig."

No one had a comment to add to that assessment.

"Forget them. They've moved on," Mallory said. "Come on in, Lauren. The water's warm. It's a great time to try skiing. RJ won't take you out far."

Lauren glanced at Ryan, waiting to see what he would say.

Ryan smiled and said, "I'll do whatever you want. You know all the signals, but Mal is right. It's a great day to learn. Very little breeze so the water is calm."

Mallory remained in the water, standing up and removing her jacket. "I'll help you. I'll stay right here and shout directions, and Nate and Cait can spot for you."

Nate couldn't have been more surprised to see Lauren stand up, strip her cover up off, and toss it down before jumping into the water.

He was damn grateful it had all happened that quickly. Seeing Lauren in a bathing suit had almost knocked him over. If she'd turned around in front of him, he probably would have flipped backward out of the boat.

Damn, but she was gorgeous and built.

She wore a navy blue one-piece suit with white bands at the edges. Most women under thirty wore bikinis, but she couldn't have chosen a better suit to accentuate her curves. Where had she been hiding her breasts?

It occurred to him that she'd probably purchased it to hide as much skin as possible—another sign of whatever trauma she'd been through.

His gaze was glued to her willowy form as she swam over to the ladder at the end of the dock and climbed up.

Now he had the full rear view. Nice ass, nice everything. He released the breath he'd been holding and ran his hand down the front of his face.

Ryan smirked and said, "Patterson, you all right?"

Hell, he'd noticed. Nate just said, "Yeah, fine." Then he muttered, "Damn."

Ryan had just taken a sip of water, and he spat part of it out as he laughed, glancing back at Nate.

"Sorry," Nate said.

Ryan whispered, "Hey, she's not my sister. She's my stepsister, and a new one at that. I noticed."

Cait turned around to glare at Ryan, and he just reached over to pull her close for a kiss. She laughed after the kiss and pushed him away. "Leave it to Nate, Ramsay."

Nate tossed the tow rope out to Mallory, who brought it over to Lauren while Ryan positioned the boat. Once Lauren was wearing the gear and in position to ski, Mallory stood off to the side and gave Ryan a thumbs up. He took off, and Nate watched as Lauren held the tow rope with a death grip, struggling to stand up straight on the skis. She lost her balance and fell gracefully into the water, but Ryan maneuvered back in front of her while she climbed out and got into position on the dock. Mallory gave her pointers on what to do differently, then she gave it another try.

Hell, he could do this all day, watch that lithe beauty climb out of the water and up the ladder. She had the longest legs he'd ever seen, and every time she stepped out of the water, he held his breath as if he were afraid she'd disappear. He forced himself to change his thoughts, or he'd have to jump in the water to calm his erection.

Lauren persevered, and he was glad to see her commit. On her fourth attempt, she was finally able to stand up strong and hang on to the rope, and they all cheered her on as Ryan gunned the motor a little bit and took off out of their cove and into the lake. He did his best to avoid any big wakes and Lauren held on strong. Just as he took a wide turn to head back toward their property, the same boat they'd encountered earlier emerged from a spot near shore and drove up behind Lauren.

Adrenaline shot through Nate. "Ryan, take her in. Those ass-holes are going to taunt her. I can see she's tensed up."

Ryan didn't say anything but he changed his course, keeping his eye on both directions. The second boat came in too close, like before, then turned off to the side and gunned it, sending a huge wake at Lauren that tossed her into the air and into the water. She let go of the rope and went under.

Nate wanted to dive in after her, but the life vest she wore brought her up to the surface quickly. She coughed and sputtered a bit and then swam toward the two skis that had popped off her feet. Ryan drove the boat in a circle around her, pulling in so he could make sure she was all right.

"You want to go again, or have you had enough?"

Lauren shook her head and pointed to the boat. "I've had enough."

Ryan cut the engine and dropped the ladder over the side so she could climb into the boat. Nate helped with the skis, getting them inside, then offered her his hand.

This time she didn't hesitate to accept his help. She came up out of the water like a goddess, her hair wet and slicked back, the water sliding down all the parts of her body he wished to explore. Cait handed her a towel that she wrapped around herself.

"That was great until the assholes came up behind you," Ryan said, grinning at her.

Cait added, "Yeah, you got up strong. I've never seen you do so well. Nice job. How did it feel?"

"Great until I heard the engine behind me." She plunked down on one of the cushioned benches, wrapping the towel more tightly around her. "Was it the same boat as before? I was afraid to look."

Ryan nodded, searching the area for the group as he reeled in the tow-line.

Nate said, "Ramsay, if you see them, I think we need to have a conversation with those boys."

Ryan nodded and glanced at him before he returned to the driver's seat, the expression in his eyes mirroring the rage in Nate's gut.

They needed to find those bastards.

CHAPTER FIVE

LAUREN CLOSED HER EYES, THINKING about how frightened she'd been when that boat had come up close to her. She could also swear she'd heard someone shout to her, but she couldn't make out the words. Now she'd be suspicious of everything and everyone.

She shivered in the wind, and Nate grabbed another towel and wrapped it around her shoulders. "Thank you," she mumbled, chastising herself immediately for having run off on him earlier. He was a nice guy. She should try to talk to him more, actually make friends. She could handle being friends with him.

That's exactly what her counselor had encouraged her to do—make friends with more males. She thought it would help Lauren to trust men again. True, she had many wonderful men in her family, but it was hard to trust new people. No, new *men*.

She glanced at Nate out of the corner of her eye. He was so good-looking—tan and muscular in all the right places, with just a smattering of dark hair across his chest. She wondered how often he went to the gym to work out. *Quit it, Lauren, that's not the kind of question a friend asks.*

She thought he was staring at her, but she couldn't tell through his sunglasses. He moved his gaze to the shoreline, then bolted out of his seat. "Right there, Ramsay." He pointed toward a boat just pulling away from a dock.

Ryan looked in that direction and turned the wheel to steer the boat toward them. The two crafts were headed straight for each other, though not at top speed.

Cait put her hand on Ryan's shoulder. "Is he going to play chicken with you? Please don't, Ry. Those games scare me."

"No, he's going to listen to what I have to say. They're a threat to anyone on this lake, and some people could have young kids on board." Once they drew close, Ryan blew his horn and slowed his engine to a crawl, drawing up next to the other boat. Nate was on the side closest to them.

Ryan shouted, "Allow me to teach you proper boating etiquette. There's a certain distance you should keep between your vessel and a person in the water, whether they're skiing or not."

Dom was still driving the boat. "Ramsay, your word means nothing out here on the water. You're not coast guard, last I heard."

His crew laughed at the joke, and he gave Ryan a huge smile.

Nate jumped to his feet, and something about his stance told her he was barely keeping a handle on his temper. "You were too close to our skier and she fell because of your wake."

"That's her problem, not ours," piped in a guy with a beer gut and a black eye.

"You mean Lauren huddling back there?" Dom pointed to her, and she couldn't help but shrink away. "I can't help it if she can't ski."

Trevor said, "Leave her out of it, guys."

"Shut up, Hutton," Dom shouted. "We're going. Teach her to ski, Ramsay."

Nate said, "Move your boat a little closer, and I'll teach you not to yell at a lady."

"I don't see a lady," the one with the beer gut scoffed.

Nate said, "Bring me closer, Ryan."

Beer Gut drawled, "And you think you can take five of us?"

"Yeah, I do. Come closer, and I'll take you out first, you piece of shit. I'll take you by the neck and toss you overboard before I go after the rest."

Beer Gut, a.k.a. Randy, moved away from the edge of the boat, edging behind one of his friends. The rest of his crew laughed at him. Nate was larger than anyone in their boat, and much more muscular. But there were five of them. He couldn't possibly win a fight with those odds.

She whispered, "Please don't, Nate."

Dominic gunned his engine and brought his boat around to the other side. Once he was close enough, he whistled. "It's nice to see Lauren Grant in the flesh. You don't come out too often, do you?

Drop the towel, Lauren. Give us a good view."

Lauren stood between the boat and Nate. She backed up until she hit Nate's chest. He immediately wrapped an arm around her waist, and to her surprise and pleasure, the touch felt good—comforting, not scary. She pushed closer to him. "Please don't, Nate. Let them go."

Randy said, "Yeah, please don't, Nate. You'll only get hurt." His voice had climbed up two octaves in imitation of hers. The tone of his voice went up the back of her neck, causing goose bumps to break out down both arms.

She shivered and Nate stepped in front of her, shielding her from view. He was so tall and his shoulders were so massive, she couldn't see past him.

She didn't *want* to—instead she closed her eyes and wished they were back at the dock.

Nate said, "You insult her one more time, and I'll jump into that boat to kick your ass." His voice had dropped to a dangerous register and silence reigned on both boats.

Ryan said, "We're leaving. Don't follow us, Dominic. I may not have my badge out here, but I know who to call about a boatful of drunks on the water."

"Big man, Ramsay," Randy shouted. "Go on home."

Ryan turned the boat away, forcing Lauren to grab Nate's arms to keep from falling. He spun around, laying gentle hands on her shoulders, and said, "Sit down over here, Lauren. Don't let the assholes bother you."

Little did he know that was impossible for her.

Ryan headed back in toward their boathouse. "We can go out later if you like, but I promised Lorraine we wouldn't miss the food. She puts on quite a spread."

Nate added, "If you want anything at all, you better get there before Tristan eats. We eat take-out most of the time, so we're all excited for some home cooking."

Lauren said, "My mother's cooking is the best. I think Tristan will be happy."

They pulled into the dock, and Lauren was happy to be on dry land again, safe from the jerks in the other boat. Even so, she found herself wanting to stay close to Nate. She grabbed her cover-up and leaped onto the dock. "Introduce me to your brothers?" she asked as they headed up the slope at the back of the house.

"Sure. In fact, I see the two of them in line for the buffet. Are you hungry?"

"Yes. I love my mother's summer spreads."

Once they moved through the buffet on the porch, Nate and Lauren joined Tristan and Sam at an outside table on the patio. They exchanged a quick round of introductions, and Lauren settled her napkin on her lap and lifted her gaze across the table, only to freeze when she noticed Tristan's plate.

Nate grinned, so he must have noticed her reaction.

"What?" Tristan said through a mouthful of macaroni salad. "We don't get good food like this very often." He finished chewing, then said, "Nate makes a great breakfast and Sam makes spaghetti with a jar of sauce and frozen meatballs, but that's it. I had to try everything." He dove into a pile of salt potatoes with his fork.

Lauren couldn't help but giggle as she looked at the two heaping plates of food in front of the teenager. "Can you really eat all that?"

Nate and Sam answered in unison. "Yeah."

They all burst into laughter just as Mallory walked by. "Wow." She whistled. "Whose plate is that?" She was staring at Tristan's second plate, mounded with salads and side dishes, which sat almost in the middle of the table.

The group pointed at Tristan, who shrugged and gave them a Cheshire-cat grin.

Mallory asked, "May I sit?" as she grabbed the empty chair. "I have to see this go down. I'll make sure and tell Lorraine if you finish it all."

"I will," he mumbled through a bite of a hot dog. He frowned as if he couldn't believe she'd questioned his persistence.

"Join us," Nate replied. "Mallory, this is my brother, Sam, and the one with all the food is Tristan."

Tristan stood up and gave a mock bow since his mouth was full.

Lauren grinned at him. "A hot dog, a cheeseburger, and a pulled pork sandwich?"

Tristan nodded as he took a bite of his cheeseburger. "And don't forget all of the sides."

Sam said, "You'd think we never feed him, but he's eaten like this ever since he started working out at the gym."

Tristan stopped for a moment, took a deep breath and said, "This is great. Tell your mom the potato salad is excellent, and that green stuff with the pistachios in it is even better."

Lauren couldn't help but laugh again. "I will." All of the brothers looked alike, but Tristan and Nate shared the same dark hair and gray eyes. Sam's coloring was lighter, and his eyes were brown.

Her gaze caught Nate's, and a bolt of pleasure shot straight to her core.

Nate's phone went off, so he grabbed it. "Excuse me," he said as he stepped away from the table. A minute later he returned and said, "Sorry, but I'm on call. Working house fire on the other side of town. Got to go. Thanks so much, Lauren and Mallory. Thank your mom and Ryan for inviting me." He stepped away and turned to his brothers, "See you at home later." He reached back to grab his hot dog to take with him.

Sam said, "If you need me, call. I haven't had a beer yet."

Nate nodded and left, trotting across the lawn to his truck.

Lauren felt like she'd lost something important.

❧

Three days later, Lauren parked her car in the library parking lot, glancing around before she got out to make sure there was no one that appeared threatening lurking around. The weekend had helped restore her, and she had classes the next day, so she wanted to do a bit of research. While her favorite old tomes were at the library at Cornell University, there were several useful books on Scottish history at the Summerhill College's library.

For a long time after her first attack, she'd sworn to never go out alone again, but she'd woken up one day and decided she would not let the bastard beat her. She was too strong for that.

This last attack had been different. Though her life had been threatened, it didn't feel as personal. Ryan seemed convinced that the arsonist's purpose had been to convince her to end her group.

And so she had stopped it. For now. Her brothers and stepfather had convinced her it was the best course until things settled down. The group met twice a month, so she'd only had to cancel one meeting so far, and she had honestly blamed it on her health. She was not up to handling others' issues when she was afraid for her own safety. At least she could refer them to Stacy's Center, though the distance would be tough for some.

Lauren was tired. For the moment, anyway, she'd had enough. Her stepfather had warned her that dealing with traumatized women would wear on her, that she would need to take extra-special care of herself to stay strong enough to be of assistance to others. He'd been right, so right. For the time being, she just wanted to study and forget about all her troubles—and everyone else's. Sure, she knew it sounded selfish, but she was drained. The fire had taken a lot out of her.

She'd seen many counselors, so she knew the warning signs of being pulled back under the cloud of depression—too much sleeping, too many tears, and too much solitude. She'd felt herself pulling away from her family lately, which had frightened her enough to force her to take action. So she'd vowed to get out to her safe places. Skiing had been great for her and, much to her surprise, Nate's company had also been a welcome balm. She wished their relationship would go further, but she knew it wouldn't be fair to him, so she shoved that thought to the back of her mind.

There were other, easier, ways of pushing herself to step outside her comfort zone. One was getting well so she could once again help the women in her group. First on her list was the library, and she promised herself she would speak to at least two people while there. Her fingers still gripped the steering wheel, but she managed to release them one finger at a time.

Take a deep breath, Lauren. You can do this.

A second spot check assured her there was no one in the area. It was still daylight, and it was early in the week. She had her phone, her mace, and her brothers and stepbrothers had taught her how to fight back.

That was something she hadn't done the first time. She'd been paralyzed with fear.

Taking a deep breath, she pulled out her keys and reached for the door handle. As she opened it wide and glanced around, she felt her body react in the usual way—racing pulse, sweaty palms, shallow breathing. She fought through it, making herself stand up, grab her bag, close the door, lock it, check the lock again, and turn around. One foot at a time....*one step at a time.*

Deep breath.

She dropped the keys in her bag, checked to make sure she had her phone.

Fifty steps. Ten more. Five more. She could almost let her breath out.

Whoosh. She opened the library door and stepped into the foyer. A calming sensation entered her body and she smiled. She'd done it.

Moving inside the old stone building, she took a deep breath to inhale one of her favorite smells—that of old books. There were shelves, racks, and piles of books everywhere. Books were her sanctuary, offering her a welcome escape from the world she lived in.

She had two favorite genres—history books, especially from the medieval time period, and historical romance. Though she'd once been ashamed of her love of romance, she now felt differently. Reading romance novels at night helped her sleep. It freed her, temporarily, of the nightmares. There was such a wealth of time periods in historical romance. Scottish historicals were her favorite because of her family's heritage, and she loved the medieval time period, but she often read novels set during the Revolutionary War, the American Civil War, or World War II. Her only complaint about books was that she didn't have time to read all of them.

Her Bachelor's degree was in history, and she had originally planned to become a high school history teacher, but now she was pulled in another direction. She'd fallen in love with the 1200s of Scotland, the time of lairds and chieftains, of clan wars, skirmishes, and more. Whenever she found any book about that time period, she would get lost in the medieval world, not realizing how much time had passed while she read.

Then she'd discovered the Battle of Largs and she couldn't soak enough information on the period. She'd decided to make it the subject of her master's thesis. Taking a deep sigh of satisfaction, she strolled over to the desk and whispered, "Hello, Mrs. Evans."

The woman behind the desk in a pencil skirt, her hair up in a tight bun with the requisite pencil behind her ear, spun around and said, "Lauren Grant! Thank goodness, you're here. I haven't seen you in such a long time. I heard about your house being burned down, you poor thing."

People had started to turn their heads and stare, but Lauren knew it was only because they were talking in the library, a place where everyone sought peace and quiet. Sandy Evans said, "Never mind. I'm glad to see you. Call me sometime. Can I help you with anything?"

Lauren shook her head. "Not today. I have some research to do, so I'm going upstairs. I'll catch you on the way out." Summerhill College and Cornell University had reciprocal library privileges for their students.

She waved to the older woman and headed up the large staircase in the middle of the library, glancing down at the various cubicles tucked into the corners for studying. They weren't very busy tonight, though it was still the beginning of the semester. By finals week, every cubicle would be taken with students trying to cram a semester's worth of information into their heads in one or two nights. School libraries, while losing some to internet searches, still thrived. Many students required silence when they studied, and it wasn't possible in the dorms, or in the Grant-Ramsay abode.

She settled into her favorite spot, texted her mother to let her know she'd arrived safely, and then moved down the aisles of books, searching for some of her favorite books about the 1200s of the Highlands of Scotland and clan wars.

She'd found many references to Clan Grant and Clan Ramsay in different time periods, but very little back in the 1200s, mostly because so little had been recorded back then. While she had no idea if she was a descendant of Clan Grant, she loved the thought. She found the fact that her mother had married a Ramsay so delightfully coincidental that she was determined to seek out all the information she could on the two clans.

As one Scottish historian had told her, there hadn't been many major events during the 1200s in the Highlands to record until the Battle of Largs.

The battle wasn't well known, mostly because nothing decisive resulted from the battle until much later. Lauren had pored over online documents and found enough basic information to recreate the battle. The Norse had plundered and pillaged up the coastline, ravaging the Scottish women and stealing anything of value. The two sides had met in battle in Largs. The Scots had fought hard, sending the Norse, now known as the Vikings by many, back onto their galley ships and down the firth to the Norse King Haakon on the Isle of Arran. The King of the Scots had hoped to wrest control of the Western Isles of Scotland back from the Norse as part of the spoils of the surprise victory, but the King of Norway didn't relinquish them for two more years.

It seemed a bit curious to her that despite the acrimonious relationship between the Norse and the Scots there were statues in Ayr celebrating the Vikings and their culture. It was a little bit curious to her. She found a couple of books to peruse, so she settled down, her laptop open to record her notes as she searched.

Before she knew it, someone made an announcement that the library was closing. She glanced at her watch in shock, unable to believe it was almost eleven p.m. She hadn't planned on staying past nine, but she'd gotten so wrapped up in the history of Clan Grant she'd lost track of time.

Now it was pitch dark out...

She could do it. There would be others in the parking lot. She would not be alone.

She packed up, making sure everything was saved on her laptop, and returned the books she'd looked over to the right place for reshelving. Checking her phone, she was surprised to see a text and a voice message from Nate. Once she made it to her car and locked the door, she'd check them both. Maybe she'd even call him just to calm her nerves...and also because she wanted to talk to him.

As she walked down the staircase, she glanced around, hoping to see others getting ready to leave. Ryan had advised her to walk out near someone, preferably someone she trusted. No one was around, so she went to the desk.

A young guy came out and said, "The library is closing. You'll have to leave."

She shifted her book bag to the other shoulder. "I know. I was just going to say goodbye to Mrs. Evans."

"She already headed out over an hour ago." He pivoted and left her there alone.

Drat. Mrs. Evans had been her last hope of finding someone to walk with, at least to the parking lot. Well, at least she wasn't parked too far back. She took a deep breath as she pressed her weight into the heavy door, enjoying the cool breeze that hit her face as soon as she stepped outside.

Pausing, she checked her surroundings as Jake had taught her and then moved quickly toward her car. She reached into her bag to grab the can of mace just in case she'd need it, but she'd remain positive.

Only about fifty steps. She would remain positive, but that didn't mean she couldn't be prepared. After opening her car door with the beeper on her keys, she reached into her bag and grabbed out her cell phone and her mace, carrying one in each hand.

Twenty, nineteen, eighteen…she spun around because she thought she'd heard a sound behind her.

No one there. A few cars were in the area, but they all looked empty.

Seventeen, sixteen, fifteen, fourteen…another sound. Nothing, but she lifted her face to the sky because she thought she'd felt a raindrop. Sure enough, it was starting to rain.

Huddling her shoulders against the damp cold, she started forward again and pulled the hood of her jacket up over her head.

Thirteen, twelve, eleven, ten…almost there.

Nine, eight, seven…almost.

Six, five…

A harsh hand shoved the small of her back, forcing her into a group of pine trees at the side of the lot. Pushing against the attacker, she attempted to turn around. To determine who'd attacked her. *The phone!* She swiped up from the bottom of her iPhone and did her best to hit the camera icon over and over again, having no idea if she was capturing anything. She screamed, but a hand quickly clamped over her mouth. Fighting as much as she could, she made sure the bastard had to drag her to get her where he wanted her. As soon as they were inside the pine trees, her vision settled on something that frightened her more than anything she'd ever seen.

Six men stood inside the trees waiting for her.

CHAPTER SIX

SIX MEN STOOD GROUPED IN a close semicircle around her. Or at least she *thought* they were men—they all had masculine figures and were dressed in dark clothing and ski masks. All the voices were deep, and she saw no breasts. She forced herself to do everything Ryan and Jake had taught her.

She screamed again, loudly enough that some sound made it through the gloved hand that covered her mouth.

Think! Mace. That's right. You have your mace. She lifted the hand still clutching the container of mace and wildly sprayed the men in front of her.

"Bitch!"

A small sense of satisfaction filled her—she'd hurt at least one of them with the spray.

"Control the bitch, would you?"

A hand came down hard on her arm, but she held onto the can, twisting it and spraying it again as soon as she saw someone's face in line with her hand. She managed to catch a third face before a fist punched her—a fist covered in a glove—hitting her with enough power for her to drop the mace.

Chaos ensued. The first man still held her from behind, his gloved hand on her face, and his other arm now held around her waist. She kicked backward and caught his shin, coming down hard on his instep.

"Ow...bitch. Here. You take her."

She was shoved into someone else's arms as several voices competed with one another.

"Is that her?"

"Yes, it's her."

"You're sure?"

"Yes, it's her."

A masked face came close to hers. The man grabbed her cheeks between his thumb and forefinger, but she twisted free of his gloved hand. He let go and yanked the glove off, reaching for her again. Something must have changed his mind, because he slapped her across the face instead, his hand moving quickly, but not so fast that she didn't notice something written on his skin. He slapped her again, this one harder than the last. "Stop. We're not going to rape you or kill you. You need to listen."

Lauren squirmed and fought, refusing to trust these men—men who would grab a woman from the library parking lot. Even as she pushed them away, panic raged inside her. Blood raced through her veins, her breath hitched over and over, and tears blurred her vision, but she would not give in to them.

Hands. Hands were all over her, opening her jacket, tearing her clothing, ripping off her bra, feeling her breasts. When she felt a hand touch her bare skin, she kicked and screamed and fought with every last ounce of energy she had.

"Hold her." The voice was that of the man who'd taken off his glove and slapped her. "Pick up her feet and toss her onto the ground."

The man who stood behind her already had control of her arms, and two others grabbed one leg each and lifted her up. They threw her down to the ground and gripped her legs, yanking them apart.

Making her totally vulnerable. *Shit, shit, shit. What do I do? Ryan? Daddy? God, please help me?*

Two hands reached up to grab her breasts, twisting her flesh until she screamed again. Someone approached her feet, so she managed to free one leg and kicked at him, connecting with bone.

"Do you three think you could control one woman? Are you tough enough to handle her?" The voice came closer, so the hands on her breasts let go. The man who'd slapped her—the leader, it seemed, came close to her face and said, "Now. It's about time you listened, bitch."

She spat at him, catching him in the eye, something that put him in a fury so fast she barely saw the fist before it hit her jaw, snapping her head to the side. A second punch hit her in the side of her head, and she saw flashes across her vision. She felt her thoughts slowing, but she fought it. She would not pass out.

"Stupid bitch!" His hand fell between her legs and he rubbed her. "Now, we'd all like a taste of you, but that isn't what we had planned for you today. The rain would make things a little messy. Hear us good. You'll put a permanent end to that group of yours. If you don't, you'll pay."

His hand moved from her crotch to her bare breast. He rubbed the outside of her skin with his bare hand, but then he grabbed her nipple and pinched it until she screamed again. "Do you understand me? No group for abused women. They ask for it. Let it die, or you'll be our next victim."

He turned his head to one of the other men and said, "Did you get that?"

She glanced into his eyes, trying to distinguish their color, but the darkness and the mask hid them well.

"If you force us, we'll all have you from every angle possible. Keep you all night long until every one of us tires of you."

He nodded his head and they let go. Some of them ran away, but three of them kicked her—two in her belly and one in her hip. She huddled into the fetal position to protect herself, but only one more kicked her in her butt. "Stay that way. If you move at all for the next ten minutes, we'll finish the job."

The scramble of feet leaving the area and hitting the pavement echoed behind her. She tried to pay attention to everything. Several car doors slammed, but only two car engines started and sped away. Why hadn't she paid attention to the makes and models of the other cars in the lot?

Calm your breathing. Think. Deep breaths, deep breaths.

Her phone. Where was her phone? It had to be close. She lay in a pool of mud, though she was mostly protected from the rain since she was under a thick oak or a maple. Not daring to stand yet, she lifted her head to check her surroundings for her phone, but she couldn't see it. Forcing herself to slide on the ground so it wouldn't appear she was moving, she ran her hand in the mud. Tears flowed freely now, and her belly hurt from the kicks to her abdomen. Her head pounded, but she needed to find the phone. Nothing. Shivers racked her body, a sign of shock. This she knew from experience, because it had happened to her the first time. Mallory had told her shock was real and it was bad.

She had to stay alert, get help. She propped herself up on her elbow, glancing to see if anyone was around, but the area looked empty. Did she dare scream? Had one of them stayed behind to watch her?

Deciding to take the chance, she screamed, "Help me! Please, someone help me. Call 911."

No response. The area was quiet and deserted. She maneuvered into a different position so she could lengthen her reach, and her hand fell on something hard.

Her phone. Sobbing now, she sat up. The rain drove down harder, but she gripped her phone in her hand, swiping at the screen to see it. She had to wipe it on her jacket several times before she could even determine how to turn in on. When it lit up, she cried with gratitude.

The simple task of hitting the contacts button took her several tries. Her vision blurred, her hand shook. She had trouble focusing on her task, but she would not give up. Finally, she found the contact numbers and hit R for Ramsay. Ryan's name popped up, so she texted him.

Help me library.

Then, after several more mishaps, she found the keypad and dialed 911.

The last thing she remembered was hearing a car pull into the parking lot.

CHAPTER SEVEN

NATE HAD WORKED A QUIET Monday after the holiday weekend, his thoughts returning again and again to Lauren Grant. He wanted to reach out to her, but she'd made it clear she wasn't ready for a relationship. The last thing he wanted to do was freak her out.

He deliberated the matter over and over, and finally decided to call her on Tuesday night. His call went straight to voicemail, so he left her a message. He texted her, too, hoping maybe she'd just turned her phone off in the library or something.

Was it true that the only places she went were the library and school? It made him sad to think about it—she had so much to give the world. She was like a bright light. He turned on the television, figuring he could distract himself with a game, but he had trouble focusing. Something was bothering him.

Sam sat on the end of the couch, grabbing the remote from him and finding a college game. "What the hell is wrong with you? You keep fidgeting."

"I don't know." He brushed his hand across the stubble on his chin.

They watched a few more plays, and Sam said, "You're doing it again."

"I know. I can't help it."

"What's her name?"

Nate sighed. "Lauren Grant."

"The one from the picnic? I can't blame you. She's nice—and a looker—but don't let the captain know. She was your victim."

"I know, but it's easy to explain how I ran into her. Ryan and I are friends, and he invited us to that picnic."

Sam nodded. "She's quiet," he said, "but there's something about her. She seems confident, yet I get the impression she's not confident at all."

"Yeah, I picked up the same vibe. She's kind, beautiful, sexy... you name it, but she's troubled. And I don't think it's just from the arson."

"Troubled? Why?" Sam stuffed a few more chips in his mouth.

"She started a group for abused women at Summerhill College. I think it's personal for her."

Sam's mouth still full, he managed a garbled, "Oh." When he finished chewing, he asked, "Are you sure it's a good idea to pursue her?"

"No, but I can't stop thinking about her." He bolted out of his seat and started pacing, needing an outlet for his nervous energy. The thought—*something wrong, something, wrong, something wrong*—kept cycling through his head. Finally, the words came out. "Something's wrong."

"What?"

"She's an introvert by her own description, hardly goes anywhere other than school and the library, but she hasn't answered my call or my text."

"So? Maybe she's not interested in you, hot shot." His brother gave him a sideways grin.

"Oh, screw you. I'm going to check on her. I'll be back soon." He grabbed his keys and his jacket, threw his phone in his pocket and moved out to his truck, just noticing that it was starting to rain.

He drove by her parents' house on the lake, but her car wasn't there. While he sat at a traffic light, he texted her again. Still no answer. Where else could she be? She claimed she only went to classes and the library, and it was way too late for her to be in class.

He decided to check the library, so he pulled into the parking lot and drove through it, searching the area. There was one car still parked there, but he couldn't tell for sure if it was hers.

When he pulled closer, the discomfort he'd felt all evening burst into full bloom in his belly. It was her car. He pulled into the lane and noticed something next to the car. A book bag or a purse. Something that didn't belong in the middle of the road. He parked next to it and picked it up. The initials LG were stitched into it, so he threw it inside his cab. He pulled his truck off to the side, then shut the engine off.

An eerie quiet hit him. It was totally dark and deserted except for her car and the lights in the parking lot. The sound of the rain hitting the asphalt echoed in his mind as he ran to the side of her car to see if she'd made it inside.

She had not. He searched the ground as he walked away from the car, his gaze catching on something in front of him. He bent over to see what it was.

Shit. Her keys. They had to be hers. He hit the button, and sure enough, the locks engaged in her car.

He followed the sidewalk to the now closed library building—no sign of her—then turned around to follow it back. Pulling his phone out, he was ready to dial 911, but then he heard something. He retraced his steps back toward her car, just then noticing a copse of trees off to the side. As he came closer, he thought he heard a small moan.

Shoving branches aside, he saw a beaten body on the ground. His heart leapt to his throat. It was Lauren, and someone had hurt her.

He dialed 911 and gave his location. The operator's immediate response was that a unit had already been dispatched. Hoping the unit would arrive soon, he knelt in the mud to make sure she had a pulse, silently praying that she hadn't been badly injured. Who the hell would hurt an innocent like Lauren? The hood of her jacket was up, and she lay in a pool of mud, her phone clutched in her hand. Pushing the hood back a touch, he touched her cheek, relieved to feel it was still warm, and then reached in for her carotid pulse on her neck.

At the same moment he felt her pulse, he heard a shallow but definite breath. "Lauren? It's me, Nate."

The rain pelted around them, and he heard the distant wail of a siren. She picked her head up for an instant and opened her eyes, but then her head fell back again.

"Lauren? Stay with me, hon. Please?"

He cupped her cheeks with his warm hands, trying to give her his heat, anything. His training told him not to move her, but it was at war with his desire to scoop her up and take her to his truck. "Lauren? Where are you hurt?"

She opened her eyes again, a dazed expression on her bruised face. "Hurt? Where?" he prompted again.

She patted her belly. That movement hit him like a baseball bat to his head. How had he not noticed her torn clothes before? Her sweater was ripped, her bra ruined. He managed to find the zipper on her jacket and closed it up.

"Where are you hurt besides your belly?"

"They kicked me." With a burst of energy that came out of nowhere, she pushed up to a sitting position, swinging and flailing her arms at her assailant. "Leave me be. Go away, all of you. Leave."

She screamed and swung, so Nate did the only thing he could do. He sat in the mud beside her, tugged her onto his lap, and held her. "Lauren, it's Nate. They're gone, and they won't touch you anymore. I've got you. I can see a police car coming into the parking lot. The EMTs will be here soon."

She stopped flailing, turned her gaze to him, and whispered, "Nate?"

"Yeah. I've got you. They're gone."

Her head fell against his shoulder and she snuggled against him. He could feel tremors overtake her, so he just held her. "Who?" he asked, so he could kill the bastard himself.

"I don't know."

"One man?"

She shook her head.

"How many?"

"Six. No, seven."

"Did you see them?" The police car pulled up behind his truck and the officer got out, gun drawn.

"Masks." Her eyes closed again.

"Officer?" he yelled. "In the trees, but I can't move. Unarmed. Nate Patterson, firefighter."

Ryan Ramsay stepped cautiously inside the trees and then ran toward him. "Lauren? Is that her, Patterson?"

"Yeah, she's in bad shape. Clothing torn, bruised face and abdomen, heart rate 110, respirations 18, shallow. Maybe going into shock. Shivering."

"What happened?" He tipped his head back to listen to his radio. Nate heard the response: "ETA, three minutes."

"I don't know. I tried to call her, text her, but she didn't answer.

Had a bad feeling, so I came to the library to see if she was here. Found her bag on the ground near her car, her keys in the middle of the road. Heard her moan and came in here."

"Why did you move her?"

"She sat up and tried to punch me," he said, stroking her back in a soothing motion. "Fighting pretty hard."

"Scared?"

"Scared shitless. All she said was there were seven of them."

"Seven?"

"First she said six, then she corrected herself—seven of them, all masked."

Ryan said, "Someone held her, she could only see six."

"You're fast, Ramsay. I just called 911."

"I called it in, too. Turns out they had a call from her phone, but she didn't speak. She texted me. I was out on a call, but I came here as soon as I saw her message." Ryan pulled Lauren's hood back, revealing the bruises on her face.

Ryan said, "Son of a bitch." She had a large goose-egg on her temple. "Was she raped?"

"I noticed her sweater and bra were torn, so I zipped her jacket closed. Her pants were on. She didn't say the word about any sexual abuse, but she says they kicked her."

Nate wanted to say, "I'll kill the bastards." But he kept it to himself.

☾

Lauren woke up to voices. She was in some sort of a room, but she didn't know where. Then it all came back to her. She'd been attacked on her way out of the library. Her gaze shifted around the room. Ryan, her brother Spencer, and Nate.

Her gaze stopped when it reached Nate, her savior. His face was the first one she remembered seeing after the assault. Why had he gotten there before Ryan or the EMTs?

She didn't care—she was just happy to see him. How she wished he'd hold her in his arms, just like he'd done in the rain.

Spencer was clearly the on-call physician tonight. He had his lab coat on, and as soon as she stirred, he hurried over to her bedside. "Lauren, can you tell me where you are?" He pulled out a penlight and shined it in each of her eyes quickly, lifting her chin to make it easier.

Her eldest brother was an emergency room doctor, so it was easy to put the pieces together. "The emergency room?" she asked. She glanced under the sheet, surprised to see she was in a hospital gown and her clothes had been removed, all but her panties.

Her brother took her hand and said, "That's right. Nate and Ryan found you. You were attacked at the library."

"My bag, my keys." She gave a half-hearted attempt to sit up, but fell back when pain arched through her body.

"Don't worry about anything," Spencer said. "Nate has them in his truck. Are you having any pain?"

"Ask her who did it," Ryan whispered.

"Health first, Ryan," Spencer responded.

Ryan grumbled that he cared about *both*, so she focused on Spencer's question. "My head hurts. Punched me…twice in the head." She knew they would ask her how her pain rated on a scale of one to ten. "Six. My belly five. My hip five. Kicked me there." She couldn't manage to get a complete sentence out.

"Any place else? I'm sorry I have to ask you this, but were you raped?"

"No."

"Okay, I'll order something for the pain. We're going to keep you overnight since you blacked out. I want to run some tests. Since you lost consciousness, I want to check to make sure you don't have a concussion. Let's also make sure you don't have any broken bones. Can you move everything? Do you think anything could be broken?"

Lauren wiggled her toes and fingers, then shook her head. "I don't think so."

He turned to Ryan and Nate. "I'm going to send the nurse in with some pain medicine. We'll need to do some tests. Check for a brain injury since she lost consciousness, make sure she doesn't have a broken hip or pelvis. She's all yours, Ryan." He kissed Lauren's forehead and left.

Just then, Jake burst in, also in uniform. "What the hell. Again, Lauren?"

Ryan motioned for him to be quiet.

"Was she the victim of the attack at the library?"

"Yes, Jake, but I'm fine. Just a little sore."

"A little? I'll beat the shit out of the bastard who did this." Jake had more of a temper than Ryan did, but it was obvious they were both worked up.

"No," was all she could manage.

Ryan whispered, "*They*, Jake. Not one bastard. Seven."

Jake stared wide-eyed at Ryan and spun around to pace. He stopped in front of Nate and asked, "Why are you here?"

"He found me behind the library," Lauren said softly. "Jake, you're making my headache worse. Please stop moving." Her hand massaged her head as she rolled to her side, the bruises on her face beginning to bother her now.

Jake halted and nodded to Ryan, sending a silent message to his brother and fellow officer.

Ryan reached for her hand and squeezed it. Lauren stared up at him, wondering how her stepbrothers, both such good men, could work around violence every day. "Who were they, Lauren?"

"I don't know. Seven men."

"Tell me what you remember."

"I did what you told me, Ryan. I fought them, used my mace, kicked and scratched. I tried to take pictures with my phone. You can check that, but there were just too many of them. I couldn't fight all seven." She reached up to tug on her hair, surprised to feel how damp and dirty it was. Bits and pieces of the night came back to her—the mud, the rain, the masks.

"You did great, Lauren. You texted me…you called 911. No one could have held it together better after what happened. What else can you tell me?" Ryan sat on a chair and pulled it closer to her.

"They said it was a message for me. They told me they'd come back for me if I don't end my support group permanently. Rape me, hurt me." She stared at the ceiling, doing her best to knock the image of seven men out of her mind.

"Did you recognize any of them? Voices? Anything?"

"No. They all had masks on. Left in two cars. It was just after eleven. Stayed too long. Shouldn't have."

"Did you have any info on the cars?"

She shook her head, tears rolling down her cheeks, tears she'd tried desperately to hold inside.

Ryan looked at Nate and asked, "Can you stay until her mother gets here? She should be here soon. I wanted to go back to campus to see if there are any frats partying, see what we can uncover before they all pass out. Since Jake is here too, we'll be able to cover the area much more quickly. With the rain, there won't be much evidence at the library."

"Sure. I'm not working in the morning."

"Thanks." He patted Nate's shoulder and kissed Lauren's cheek. "Your mom is coming. Nate will stay with you until she gets here."

Jake did the same. "Lauren, we'll find them. I promise."

With that, her stepbrothers left her and Nate alone together in the small curtained-off cubicle in the emergency room. She turned to look at him. "You don't have to stay. I'll be fine."

"I'm staying because I want to stay, and I don't expect you'll be fine for a little while. You've had too much happen to you. I wouldn't dream of leaving you alone right now." He took the chair Ryan had vacated and cocooned her hand in his warm grip.

She stared at Nate, wondering why he would be so kind to a near stranger—surely he knew better than to want to date her now—but decided to accept it. But then something occurred to her. "How did you know I was there? Or did you find out I was here?" Her brain was cloudy, her memories unclear. Had he told her already?

"You don't remember? I came looking for you because you didn't answer my text or voicemail."

She frowned, doing her best to bring the memory back, but it wouldn't come. Her hand massaged her forehead, trying to summon it from the depths of her tired brain. Deciding it didn't matter, she said, "Thank you." She felt so cold, she didn't know what to do. When she started to shiver, she finally turned to Nate and asked, "Blanket. Please?"

Nate glanced around the small area, then took one look at her and sighed.

She brushed away the tears that had started to fall. "Sorry. I can't stop the tears."

Nate shook his head. "No, that's not it. I don't see any blankets." He opened the curtain, probably looking for any attending nurses who could help. She heard him talk to an aide, asking if he could move her, then he returned after the aide gave him permission. Moving decisively, he wrapped her IV cord over his shoulder, scooped her up into his arms, and sat back in the chair, wrapping his muscular arms around her. "I'll warm you." He rested his jacket across her lap, covering her legs as best he could.

She shuddered as Nate's heat spread over her. The man was like a roaring fire on a cold night at the lake. Not caring what anyone thought, she rested her head on his shoulder and closed her eyes, inhaling his familiar scent, though she could tell his hair was still wet from the rain. Or was it her own hair she smelled? Nate comforted her like no other—she wasn't sure why, but that was the plain and simple truth of it—and she decided to enjoy him. "I warned you," she whispered, her hand gripping his shirt as if she could keep him there by that simple gesture.

"About what?"

"Being a burden." Just the words brought tears to her eyes.

"You're not a burden. I quite like having you on my lap, and you weigh as much as a feather. I'm sorry this happened to you, that I didn't get there sooner." He rubbed his thumb across the skin on her arm.

"Me, too. Now I'll be worse." Three attacks. Would she ever be able to put them behind her?

"I don't understand."

She heaved a big sigh. How could she explain it? "I want to hide from it all. That's why I don't go anywhere. Didn't want to put myself at risk...and they hurt me anyway."

"You can't stop living your life."

"But I will. Now I'll be afraid of the library and worse..."

"Worse?" He rubbed his hands across her forearms, left uncovered by the short-sleeved hospital gown.

A patient care assistant came in with a basin full of warm water and a washcloth. She seemed a little caught off guard to find Lauren wrapped up in Nate's arm, but she recovered quickly and pointed to Lauren's face. "For the dirt. I'll wash it off."

"No," Lauren barked as she lifted her head. "It...it hurts too much." In truth, she could not stomach the thought of having a stranger touch her. She'd try on her own when she was ready, but she just didn't care at the moment. The dirt could stay put for now. The woman stood there staring at her, waiting for her to comply or suggest some sort of solution, but she was just too weary to do anything. To say anything.

"I'll leave it here with a bar of soap. You can do it yourself if you'd rather. But you should get the dirt off those small cuts. Oh, and your nurse said she'll be in with your medication in a few minutes." She left and drew the curtain closed behind her.

Lauren's head fell back onto Nate's shoulder.

He picked the cloth up and dipped it into the warm water. "Here. I'll help you."

She lifted her head and let him. True, she could do it herself, but decided she'd rather have him do it since he had offered. Strangely, she trusted him to do it. Peering into his gray eyes, she said softly, "This is above and beyond the call of duty for a firefighter."

He chuckled, squeezing the excess water out of the cloth. "Maybe, but I don't have anything else to do tonight. The football game was boring. It was college, not my favorite to watch."

"Who's your team?"

"The Bills, of course. They don't play until Sunday. Do you watch football?" He ran the cloth across her forehead first.

"Yes. My stepfather is the biggest Bills fan of all. And my mother's become a fan, too."

Nate had the gentlest touch possible. He used the warm cloth to wash her face, down her neck, even her hands and her arms. It felt so good to let him take care of her. To let someone else bear the burden for a moment. She'd been alone for such a long, long time.

"Do you want to tell me about it?" He rinsed the cloth again, then worked on the back of her neck, something that caused her to moan with pleasure.

"Tell you about how scared I was or how nasty they were? Or should I tell you how hard it is to stand near a man I don't know for fear their hands will reach out and do what any of those bastards did to me? They groped and pulled and punched and shoved and pinched me, and I was powerless to stop them. I tried everything Ryan and Jake showed me…"

"And?"

"The mace. I even got a few of them with it."

He set the cloth back into the basin and ran his thumb across her bottom lip. "So you hurt them, too."

"I did." She did her best to recall any other details. "You know, I think I kicked a couple of them."

"Well done," he whispered, an inch away from her mouth. Somehow it wasn't frightening that Nate was this close to her. She wanted him to kiss her. As if he could read her thoughts, he gave her a chaste kiss and then pulled back so their lips were almost touching. "You fought well. Two or three big men couldn't control you. Few people could have done better."

She brought her hand up the side of his neck, barely touching him. She actually touched the pads of her fingers to his skin, willingly, and he kissed her again. He tasted wonderfully and strangely familiar, and familiar was something she needed more than anything right now.

The nurse from before came in and said, "Dr. Grant asked me to bring this in for your pain. Can you state your name and date of birth, please?"

She did, and accepted the pill while the nurse poured a glass of water for her from the pitcher on the side table. "Thank you," she mumbled just before she let her head fall back on Nate's shoulder.

"Here's the call bell if you need anything." The nurse set in on the table next to her so it was within reach.

"Wow, you have your own brother taking care of you? That's nice."

"You know how it is in small towns. This hospital is small, so he's probably the only attending doctor tonight. He likes being on call. Says he likes being the expert." She smiled, pleased that Spencer was working tonight. He was very good at respecting her privacy, too. She peeked out through the break in the curtain to see if she could catch sight of him.

That was when she noticed her mother standing in the hallway crying.

CHAPTER EIGHT

NATE LEFT SHORTLY AFTER LAUREN'S mother arrived. He texted his brother that he'd be home in another hour, but then hopped into his truck and headed toward the college.

It was as if some gravitational pull had brought him there. He needed to know what, if anything, Ryan Ramsay had found at the frats.

Were the guys from the boat involved? There'd been five of them, including the ones Lauren and Mallory had recognized—Miller, Hutton, and Brooks. Still, wouldn't Lauren have IDed their familiar voices?

He pulled into the college's main parking lot with his truck and then climbed out and locked the door. Since Tristan was attending classes, he'd purchased a sticker for his truck, too. He'd had no idea how handy it would prove to be.

He noticed Ryan and Jake's cruisers at the front of the lot, so with any luck they'd run into each other. The college campus was set up as a rectangle, with the dorms on the outside of the quadrangle.

The college had been part of the city of Summerhill for decades, and it was always growing. In the past ten years, they'd expanded the library that Lauren loved and built two new academic buildings, one for health science and one for education.

He moved toward the center of campus before veering left, toward where the older dorms were located. Lo and behold, Ryan Ramsay was headed straight for him.

"Did you find anything, Ramsay?" Nate wished he had a couple of guys in handcuffs.

Ryan shook his head. "Not much partying tonight. First day of classes after a holiday weekend, plenty of hangovers, some of the students are just returning to campus. The two frats I visited were quiet."

"Did you see any of our friends from the boat?"

"Yeah, Dominic and Randy are in the Gamma Delta frat, but they were watching football."

"What does your gut tell you?" Nate asked.

Ryan sighed. "My gut tells me it's a fraternity that's pissed about the group she runs, especially since seven guys came at her at once. Lauren arranges self-defense classes for the women who come to her, and she's also helped assault victims seek out legal counsel through the Center her friend runs. If a frat gets associated with rape and sexual violence, it could get kicked off campus. Should be easy to find the guys if I'm right. The college only has three or four frats."

"That makes sense. I hope you find them, though if I do, I'll beat the bastards. Seven to one? That's pretty bad."

Ryan replied, "I know. I'm too emotionally involved in this. Poor Lauren. This is the third time she's been attacked. Thanks for staying with her, by the way. How did Lorraine take it?"

"She was crying when she came in, but I think it was because of how Lauren looked. I helped her wash up, but just her face and hands. Her hair was still a mess, and you can't hide the mud in her hair. Once Lauren spoke to her, she calmed down. The good thing was that the pain medicine they gave her almost put her to sleep. Her mother said she'd spend the night there. Spencer found Lauren a private room with a lounge chair Lorraine could sleep in."

"Thanks again. I'll see you later."

"Keep me posted, Ramsay. I want those bastards. It was pretty hard finding her like that. She's pretty special." He stuffed his hands in the pockets of his jeans, fighting the urge to turn them into fists.

Nate headed back to his truck, his mind on a pair of blue eyes full of pain as he pulled out of the lot and headed home. He pulled into his driveway and noticed Sam's truck was missing. He checked to see if he'd received any texts about his brothers leaving. Nothing.

Once inside, he found Sam sitting on the couch. It was after one a.m. "Where's Tristan?"

"He went to get something to eat. Do you want anything? Text him if you do. You might still catch him."

"What the hell? Why is he out this late? Doesn't he have an eight o'clock class?"

"I don't know." Sam cranked his head around. "What's your problem? I thought we agreed to give the kid a little more leeway. It's not Tristan's fault if that girl turned you down."

He couldn't stop himself from shouting. "No girl turned me down. Tristan better not be cutting classes tomorrow. He got a scholarship, but we're paying part of his tuition."

The door opened and Tristan sauntered in, tossing the keys on the table before he closed the door. He dropped a bag of food and two sodas on the coffee table. "Hey, Nate. How was the girl?"

"Aren't you going to class in the morning?"

Tristan smirked and said, "No. Why?"

Nate wanted to choke him. "You will go to class, or I'll kick your ass."

Tristan had the balls to ignore him. He just sat on the couch and pulled his burger out of the bag as if Nate hadn't said anything.

"Why the hell aren't you going?" Nate bellowed.

Tristan clenched his jaw and said, "Chill, brother. I don't have any classes in the morning."

Nate felt like an asshole. He sighed as he moved around to sit in the chair facing the couch. Collapsed into it and ran his hand through his hair. "Sorry about that. I just want you to do well." Why was he constantly flipping off the handle with his own brother? What was wrong with him? Sam was right. Tristan was a good kid.

"So do I, and I will, but not because you harass me about it. It'll be because I want Mom to be proud of me."

"I want Mom to be proud of you, too. You know how hard it was for me, being there, watching her die…"

"It wasn't your fault she died, Nate. Your shrink tells you that all the time."

"What the hell happened tonight?" Sam asked, chewing on the fries Tristan had bought. His eyes bored into him, seeing more than Nate would like. "I can tell something did."

He sat up, leaning his elbows on his knees. "I've been to a lot of fires, seen death, but this bothered me like nothing else."

"What?" Tristan asked through a mouthful of food.

"I found Lauren after she'd been beaten by a gang of seven guys, maybe from one of the frats at school."

"Holy shit," Sam said. "Sorry for my comment earlier."

Tristan shook his head in disgust. "If that's what the frats do for fun, I guess I'm glad I passed on rush. That's sick."

"I'm sorry for how I treated both of you," Nate said. "It wasn't right." He scratched his head, promising himself he'd channel his anger better in the future. His brothers meant everything to him, but his baggage kept getting in the way. The awful memory of losing his mother. The moment Mandy had screamed at him and walked out of his life.

He had to leave all of that behind and focus on the present moment. On protecting the people who were currently in his life.

Lauren, a voice in his head whispered, *you should have been there for Lauren.*

☾

Lauren sat in her room for two days after the fateful night at the library. She'd come home from the hospital the following day to a worried household. Her stepfather hovered over her, as did her mother, and she just wanted them all to stop. One of her classmates shared notes and assignments with her, so at least she had something to do.

Ryan had asked her countless questions, trying to trigger any new memories, but to no avail. To her dismay, the photos she'd taken hadn't revealed anything. They were all a blurry mess. She'd been given a prescription for painkillers, and while she tried not to take them, they did ease her pain. The kicks that had connected with her hip had caused the most problems. Her pelvis and hip area had swelled beyond recognition, causing her to limp, though she did her best to hide it around others. She had to take a pill before she slept, or she'd lie awake all night in pain.

She wasn't just angry at the event itself, but at the fact that the fools had left her with reminders of it. As soon as she moved a muscle in bed, she was reminded of the attack, and she hated it.

But something else niggled at the back of her mind. These men clearly want her to back down for a reason, which meant they'd either hurt women or were planning to continue hurting women. She closed the door to her room and bent down with a groan, reaching under her bed for the lock box she'd retrieved from the burned building. She opened it carefully and pulled out the chart, closing her eyes and saying a quick prayer of thanks that it hadn't been lost to the fire.

She sat at her desk and unfolded the document, careful not to tear it at the creases, flattening it so she could read it again. As soon as she determined it was still legible, she breathed a sigh of relief.

She'd started the chart after her rape, writing down all the details of the attack and categorizing everything: time of year, time of day of the attack, location of the attack, and personal characteristics of the attacker. Then she'd started the support group, and she'd begun collecting the same sort of information about the attacks made on the other women, although some of the information had been shared with her confidentially.

She took out her pen and carefully added the details of her latest attack, filling in all the details she recalled. There were times she considered giving the chart to her brother Ryan, but she'd feel like she was betraying the victims' trust. Moreover, she knew enough about the rules of privacy from the medical people in her family to know that she'd be in trouble if she relayed some of the information she'd received without permission.

Still, she continued to keep track of the details in the hopes the chart would be useful one day. Ideally, it would help her identify and catch at least some of the predators who'd hurt women. Maybe even pick up on a pattern. Ryan and Jake had other tools they could use. She only had the victims. When she had something more solid to go on, something she knew she could legally pass along, she'd talk to her stepbrothers.

Not yet. The chart was so special that she'd entered much of the information on an Excel sheet and saved it to a flash drive, needing a backup, but the electronic version wasn't as complete as the physical chart.

The sound of wheels scraping across the asphalt caught her attention. She hurried over to the window. To her surprise, the newcomer looked like Nate Patterson, her savior. She'd have to go down and thank him again.

Then she'd claim fatigue or pain and return to her room where she was safe…

Part of her wanted things to be different. She hadn't forgotten what it felt like to be encased in his arms, or to be kissed, however briefly, by his soft lips.

Folding the paper with the utmost care, she returned it to the lock box and placed it under her bed.

Her mother's voice carried up the stairs. "Lauren, Nate is here to see you." It was impossible to ignore the hope in her mother's voice—hope she'd come down, hope that she and Nate would develop some sort of a normal relationship, hope that Lauren would not go over the edge again.

She was trying—she really was. She'd gone to class today without any repercussions. Of course, despite her best efforts to cover her bruises with make-up, her professor had noticed and called her forward at the end of class.

The woman had offered her extra time for assignments, but she'd insisted she'd be able to handle everything.

"I'll be right there, Mom."

She put everything back in its place, then glanced at her reflection in the mirror. A long sigh escaped her lips. The bruising on the side of her head was still evident.

What did it matter? Nate had already seen her looking much worse.

She made her way down the staircase slowly, just to ease the pain in her hip. Fortunately, her mother and stepfather were on the enclosed sun porch with Nate. She could hear their conversation clearly.

"We were about to eat, Nate. Why don't you stay for dinner? Have a nice home-cooked meal. I made one of Lauren's favorites—macaroni and cheese. I know it's not the healthiest, but I decided she deserved something special tonight. Three and Cait will also be joining us. Oh—" she said with a laugh. "That's what Ryan's dad calls him. Same name, you know. And Paige will be there, of course." Paige, the youngest Ramsay daughter, was in her senior year of high school.

Lauren sighed, silently cursing her mother for issuing the invitation. She wasn't ready for company yet. How could she sit through an entire meal with Nate Patterson and his gorgeous eyes and his physique that begged to be touched? How could she ignore the strange push-pull she felt whenever she was in his presence?

Forcing a smile on her face, she made her way through the

kitchen and into the porch off the back, her favorite room. The sun was still out and the lake looked so calm and flat, it seemed like a person could walk across the surface and never fall in.

As soon as she stepped into the doorway, Nate hurried over to her side, offering his hand to help her step down onto the porch.

"Your hip is still bothering you?" he asked.

"Yes," she replied, wondering why he would recall such a small detail from the short time he was in the hospital with her. She took his hand and landed awkwardly, but Nate kept his smile.

As if reading her mind, he explained, "I spoke with Ryan yesterday. He told me it was the worst of your injuries."

Her mother spoke right up. "I insist you stay, Nate. I'm sure a strong man like you could use a home-cooked meal. If we have any left, I can send some home to your brothers. Do you all like macaroni and cheese?"

"We sure do. It was one of my mother's best meals. Tristan would try to eat it all."

"Well, good then. It's settled. It's a smaller group tonight, so we'll eat out here on the porch." She glanced over his head to speak to her husband. "Ryan, would you mind helping me in the kitchen, please? Lauren, settle down at the table, dear. The food will be ready in few moments. Nate will help prop your leg if you need help, I'm certain."

Lauren smiled at her mother and said, "Sure." Her attempts to set them up couldn't be more obvious, but she didn't have it in her to be mad. Her mother only wanted the best for her.

Once they were alone, she said, "Nate, thank you for all you did for me the other night. I can't thank you enough. Again."

His gray gaze warmed her, making her feel comfortable and at peace. "I'm only sorry I didn't arrive sooner."

She moved into a chair with his assistance, and he took the seat across from her. "You did more than you needed to. You stayed longer than necessary." She dropped her gaze, remembering how she'd sat in his lap while wearing nothing more than a hospital gown. Her face blushed at the thought. "Thank you for warming me up."

Being the gallant gentleman he was, he did not make an issue of it. "How are you feeling?"

"I'll be fine. It will take a few days. I made it to class today for the first time this week, so that's a good thing."

Her mother came in with a hot casserole dish full of steaming macaroni, setting it on a hot plate. Her husband set down a large wooden salad bowl before hurrying back to the kitchen, returning with salad dressing and a large loaf of fresh bread. The table had already been set for six, and an extra place setting was added for Nate.

Lauren's mom fussed over her guest like she always did. "Now I didn't bake this bread myself. I bought it at the local bakery, but it's delicious. Three told us he'd be a bit late, so let's dig in!"

Lauren's stepdad helped her mother into a chair before he sat down and said a quick prayer. They'd just begun passing the food around the table when Ryan and Cait came in through the back door, Paige right behind them.

Cait said, "Ryan heard it was mac and cheese night, so here we are."

"Lorraine, you make the best mac and cheese ever," Ryan added.

They all settled in at the table and passed the food around, chattering about everything and nothing. Paige told them about her teachers and all her classes, something Nate was able to interact with her about since Tristan had just graduated.

Lauren was pleased the others had joined them. Now she could actually sneak off to her room after dinner without offending Nate. It wasn't until the end of the meal that Nate posed a question to Ryan. "Any ideas yet?"

Ryan gave a pointed look at Lauren before he said, "We have some leads, but nothing solid yet." He changed the conversation immediately afterward.

Lauren breathed a sigh of relief. The topic had been started and ended.

Ten minutes more and she'd be alone in her room.

CHAPTER NINE

NATE COULD TELL EXACTLY WHAT Lauren had planned. Sure enough, she excused herself as soon as possible. "I think I'll go rest if you don't mind, Mom."

"Dinner was wonderful, but I'm a little tired." She pushed away from the table and headed toward the stairs.

Nate noticed the disappointment and the worry that crossed her mother's face, but she made no move to stop her. No one did.

She'd told him she feared she would retreat into herself after the attack, that she'd stop taking chances. He couldn't let her do that to herself. Not again.

He followed her to the doorway leading to the kitchen and said, "Here, allow me to help you." After he ushered her up the single step and into the kitchen, he continued to escort her to the staircase in the front room.

Lauren turned to him and said, "Thank you again for your kindness, Nate. I hope to see you soon." She took a step toward the staircase, but he stepped in front of her, barring her from taking the first step. "What are you doing?" she asked, sounding genuinely puzzled.

"I'm not going to let you do it," he whispered, wanting to keep their conversation as private as he could.

"Do what?" She crossed her arms in front of her.

"Walk away."

"I said I was tired. If you'll excuse me, I'd like to go to my room." She stared over his shoulder, refusing to look him in the eye.

"No. This isn't right for you, Lauren. You're blocking everything and everyone out—just like you said you would. If you go upstairs, you're doing it for the wrong reasons. You're doing it to hide."

"What? That's ridiculous."

He could see the fine tremor in her hand. "Are you having any serious pain at the moment?"

She quickly said, "No."

"Then take a walk with me. It's a beautiful early fall night. I'd love to stroll down to the lake, look out over the water, and watch the beautiful sunset. Would you join me, please?"

She glared at him as if she wished to choke him, but then a funny thing happened. Her eyes grew misty, and she said, "Fair enough. I'll go with you. But only for a short walk."

"Fair enough." He stepped back out onto the porch and said, "Lauren and I are going to take a stroll down to the dock. We'll be back shortly." Rather than wait for an answer, he escorted Lauren over to the front door. Once outside, he said, "Which way?"

She pointed to the right. "We can follow this walkway almost to the lake."

"Wonderful." He reached for her hand, expecting her to refuse, but she surprised him by sliding her tiny hand inside his and tucking herself a little closer to him. She wore leggings and a tunic top, the kind that hung almost to her knees. Jeans were not the material you wore over a bruised body. What she wore suited her perfectly—the simplicity only augmenting her beauty. "What's your favorite time of year on the lake?"

She relaxed against him. "Now. Everyone else prefers summer, but I love it when the lake becomes quiet and the leaves start to turn. The colors are glorious by mid-October. I love to look at the hills across the lake, see their colors shimmer when the sun is out." They walked in silence for a bit, but he noticed she slowed her pace as soon as the slope of the lawn increased. The sidewalk had ended, and they moved forward with caution.

She whispered, "Why are you doing this?"

"Quite simply because I care about you." He didn't know how else to explain it.

"Why?" She didn't look at him, but he thought she squeezed his hand a bit tighter.

He shrugged his shoulders, not sure how to answer her. They'd made it to the water, and they stepped hand in hand onto the dock that surrounded the boathouse.

"Is it because you feel sorry for me?"

He spun to face her. "No, that's not it at all. I was attracted to you before the attack at the library. There's just something about you. At the fire, I looked in your eyes, and…" Exasperation got the best of him. "I don't know why." He waved one arm, but didn't let go of her hand. "I can't always put things into words."

But maybe he could show her…

"Lauren, I'm going to kiss you because I want to, so if you don't want this, you need to stop me now."

She didn't say anything, so he took that as acceptance. He lowered his lips to hers, cupping her cheek as gently as he could. He kissed her, then stopped for a moment to see if she'd change her mind before he took her lips again, teasing her with his tongue, pleased that she parted her lips to allow him inside.

He moved as slowly as he could, not wanting to hurt her or alarm her by going too fast, but she tasted like he guessed heaven would taste—sweet, soft, accepting, and willing to duel with him a bit. He caressed her mouth with his tongue, encouraging her to share that small piece of herself with him, and so damn pleased when she did finally *did* touch her tongue to his. When had something so small ever felt this satisfying?

She winced, so he ended the kiss. "Did I hurt you?" He ran his thumb over her cheek, and her hand came up to cover his, holding him to that spot.

"No. You were so gentle. Well, the other side of my face still hurts a bit."

He pulled back a bit more to look in her eyes, surprised to see a tear there. "I made you cry. That's not a good sign."

She dropped her hand and said, "It *is* a good sign. Do you know why?"

He nodded. "It shows emotion." Something he himself was afraid to show. Had been ever since… He forced himself not to think about his mother and what had happened to her. About how it had damaged his relationships with other people.

"Yes. My counselor would be pleased. Thank you for making me come out here with you. It was wonderful. And…thank you for not giving up on me." She hugged herself, her hand coming up to hold her temple. He didn't need to ask her what she was doing. Something told him this was her way of attempting to stave off the memories she wished to forget.

He had plenty of those, so he understood.

Stop thinking about it, never think about her again, stop dwelling on what you could have done, forget the look in her eyes… Those thoughts spun through his head every day, and yet they didn't stop the memories. Not really. Maybe only time would do that.

"I don't plan on giving up on you, Lauren. Believe it or not, I understand. We'll take it as fast or as slow as you'd like."

She said, "We should probably go back."

He focused on her eyes as she stared out over the water, wondering what she was thinking. Wanting to keep her with him. "I'm in no hurry. It's beautiful out here. Stay with me for a little while?" He rubbed the back of his hand across her cheek to pull her back, or so he hoped. Returning again and again to the shadows of painful memories was not going to help her.

She startled at his touch, but a smile crossed her face as her gaze shifted back to his. This was a real smile—though a sad one—not the happy mask she put on for the world. "Since you have the time, would you mind doing something for me? You don't have to talk or anything."

Her hand released his, as if testing how the distance felt, but she almost immediately reached for him again.

"Of course. What it is?"

She stared at her feet before she lifted her chin back up, though she did not make eye contact with him this time. "Will you hold me while I cry? I don't think I can stop the tears this time."

The tears burst out before he could answer her, so he wrapped his arms around her while she clung to him, burying her face in his shoulder. She sobbed and sobbed and sobbed.

And he never wanted to stop holding her.

☾

She'd let him in when she let the tears out.

Lauren hadn't planned on allowing anyone inside. On allowing herself to need or want anyone's help. She was strong enough to battle this on her own, something she'd told her counselor—and her mother—over and over again.

But it felt wonderful to cry openly, and Nate didn't seem to mind holding her. Her wrenching sobs should have been loud enough to echo across the waters of Orenda Lake, but the inky depths absorbed them and whisked away a world of pain at the same time. The lake always seemed to calm her, its strange powers almost magical.

When the tears finally ebbed, she turned her head to the side, still resting on his shoulder, his very wet shoulder. "You're drenched," she whispered.

He chuckled, placing a gentle kiss on her forehead. Nate was as gentle and patient as any man she'd ever known. She said a quick thank you to whatever force had brought them together, though the circumstances left something to be desired.

"Did it help?" he asked.

"Yes."

"Is that the first time you've cried since the attack this week?"

"Yes. A tear has slipped out here and there, but I've always been able to contain the flood."

She picked her head up to stare at him, taking in his perfect features and the shocking warmth in his gray eyes. "Thank you. I'll bet I look a sight."

"You're always beautiful," he said, squeezing her hand.

"Now what do we do?"

He shrugged his shoulders. "It's still early. Do you need anything at the library for your classes?"

She took a step back and shook her head, a little too vehemently.

He nodded. "You need to go back. I'm offering to go with you the first time."

She thought for a moment, her mind flashing back to the trees, the bushes, and the violent shove against her back. The thought of returning to the library, her favorite sanctuary, made her skin crawl.

"You may not be ready for it yet," he said, looking into her eyes. "When you are, I'd be happy to go with you. It may take a few times before you can actually walk back in. Why don't we just drive through the parking lot, and then we can stop for an ice cream cone on the way back?"

Could she do it? Something about his confidence in her made her feel like she could handle it. She took a deep breath and nodded. "All right, but just a drive around the parking lot."

"If you change your mind, we can always head straight to the ice cream place. But it's a start." He turned to head back up the small hill and held his hand out to her.

She placed her hand in his and took a deep breath.

Yes, it was a start.

They headed out after explaining their mission to Lauren's family. Her mother appeared the most shocked, but all she said was, "Lauren, are you sure?"

She nodded. "We'll see how it goes." Her mother came over to her, so Lauren kissed her cheek and gave her a reassuring hug. "Believe me, Mom. Nate will take care of me."

Nate rested his hand on Lauren's shoulder. "I can promise you that. And if she changes her mind at any time, we'll leave immediately."

Her mother's eyes misted over as she whispered, "Thank you, Nate."

A quarter of an hour later, Nate's truck pulled into the college parking lot closest to the library. He reached for Lauren's hand and gave it a light squeeze. "You tell me what to do. I'll drive around the outside of the lot, and if you want to stop at any point, just say so. We'll leave whenever you're ready."

She nodded and gripped his hand as he started skirting the perimeter of the lot. Her eyes were glued on the side window. As he took the last curve toward the attack zone, as she'd come to think of it, her heartbeat sped up along with her breathing, but she didn't tell him to stop. She was this close to conquering one of her many fears. Sweat broke out across her forehead, and her gaze shifted back and forth between the zone and the truck's dashboard. When the truck pulled abreast of it, she tugged her hand away from Nate's and waved him on. He stepped on the gas and pulled away, causing her body to respond immediately to the decreased threat.

"Well done, Lauren. I honestly didn't think we'd get that far." He turned his head to smile at her, that full smile that reached inside her belly, causing a fluttering that was much more pleasant than the grip the zone had on her. "That was great. Are you ready for ice cream?"

She shook her head vehemently. "No. Again, please?"

He slowed his truck. "Are you sure?"

Her gaze caught his. "Yes. I need to conquer this, and I'd prefer to not be alone when it's forced on me."

"I'll bring you back another time if you'd rather."

"No. Now." She hoped he'd go along with it. "That is, if you have the time."

"I do." He turned around to head back to the spot.

She turned her head toward the zone again, forcing herself to meet the demons in her mind. She gripped Nate's hand as they pulled closer. "Slower, Nate. Please?"

He did as she asked, and as soon as they came closer, she whispered, "Stop." Her breath hitched as she stared at the location where she'd been attacked by that horrid group of men.

"You fought them, Lauren. You kicked and fought, you sprayed them with mace, you used your phone. You did everything you could, and you came out alive. You should be proud of yourself. I know I'm proud of you." His thumb caressed the back of her hand.

Voices bounced back and forth in her mind.

"Do you three think you could control one woman?"

"It's about time you listened, bitch."

Something came back to her. She peered over at Nate. "I spat on him, too."

"Him?"

"The leader. One was definitely the leader. He kept telling the others what to do. Asking them why they couldn't control me better." She opened the door.

"Whoa. I'm fine with it if you want to go over there, but not without me."

She gaped at him. His words had caught her off guard, spinning her mind away from the dark memories battling for her attention. Would he understand if she explained to him that the darkness always fought to overtake everything else in her mind? How that battle took place every day of her life?

Something unknown possessed her at the moment, some inner force or strength unleashed by this trip to the scene of the attack, and it inspired her to confront that battle head on.

Nate opened his door and hurried to her side, offering his hand to her as she climbed down from the truck, her gaze on the zone. Nate tugged her close and wrapped his arm around her.

She was grateful for his presence, for the empowering feeling of their combined strength. And she pushed herself to meet her fears head on. A few steps more and she stood on the edge of the area, much of it still trampled from her attackers and the police investigation. A chill crept up her spine as more bits and pieces came back to her, and she pushed herself to stride forward until she stood directly over the spot where she'd been accosted.

She leaned her head on Nate's shoulder as a shiver coursed through her, not a shiver of fear but one of power. The bastards would not win. She was more powerful than they thought. More powerful than them.

"It's about time you listened."

"I'm not listening," she whispered, a tear burning the corner of one eye. She lifted her head from Nate's chest to stare at him. "I'm not listening." This time it came out in a much more forceful voice.

"Good," he replied, oddly understanding what she meant. He reached up to wipe the single tear that slid down her cheek.

"I'm not listening," she yelled at him. "They need to know that." A vow curled in her gut as she continued to think about the fire and the attack—the cowards' attempt to silence her. "I'm not listening. Do you hear me, Nate?"

He smiled, encouraging her to continue. "Good. Don't allow them to control you."

"I'm not listening, I'm not listening." She brought her fists up to his chest, almost taking swing at him, but she stopped herself because this was Nate. He empowered her rather than attacked her. He wasn't one of them. "I'm. Not. Listening!"

Instead, she flung her fists over her head in triumph.

He nodded to her.

She spun around to look at the sidewalk. No one was around, so she tipped her head back and emitted a gut-wrenching bellow, ending it with the best word she could think of, "Bastards!"

She pivoted back to Nate and threw her arms around his neck. "Thank you. I'm pleased you brought me here. This was what I needed. There's only one more thing I'd like to ask of you."

He stared appreciatively at her, a wide grin on his face. "Anything. What is it?"

"Will you escort me to the library, please?"

She stepped out of the trees, her chin held high, her shoulders squared. She was done cowering. In fact, she had so much work to do, she didn't know how she could manage to get it all done.

Turning to Nate, she placed her hands on both sides of his face and kissed him hard, hoping that would let him know how much she appreciated what he'd done for her.

Now, because he'd pushed her—because she'd pushed *herself*, she had goals.

The bastards would *never* control her again.

CHAPTER TEN

NATE PULLED INTO THE DRIVEWAY of the Ramsay-Grant lake house, pleased with how the evening had gone. Lauren had confronted some of her demons, even to the point of walking into the library with him, though they had only stayed for moments. He had felt her pulse speed up when they left the library to walk to his truck, but she hadn't so much as increased her pace. He thought she'd come a long way in one trip.

As soon as they pulled in, Ryan came out of the house, headed straight toward them.

Lauren said, "I didn't expect Ryan to still be here."

Ryan nodded to them, but he waited for Nate to get out of the truck and help Lauren down before he spoke. "Hey, I hope you had a successful trip."

"We did," Nate replied. "Lauren actually walked into the library again."

Ryan stared at her, wide-eyed. "That's an accomplishment you should celebrate."

"I agree," Lauren said. "I can't thank Nate enough for going with me. But why are you still here? Is anything wrong?"

"No. Actually, I was hoping to speak with you before I left. I didn't want to bring up your case during dinner. It's up to you if Nate stays to listen. Cait's doing the dishes for your mom."

Lauren glanced at Nate and said, "It's fine with me, but if you have to go, I'll understand."

Nate didn't hesitate in his response. "I'll stay."

Ryan pivoted and led them into the backyard. "We can talk on the back porch."

They followed Ryan out to the large expanse. Lauren's mother and stepfather were back on the porch, though they'd relocated to the comfortable lounging area. Lauren chose a chair near her mother, so he took the chair next to her.

Ryan faced them all, but before he brought up the investigation, he started by congratulating Lauren on her accomplishment. "Lorraine, Nate took Lauren to the library. She actually walked inside and over to the area she was attacked."

Lorraine looked like a heavy load had been lifted off her shoulders. "Nate, I cannot tell you how much we appreciate your help. Lauren, how are you doing? That was a big step."

"I'm fine. It was difficult at first—" she reached for Nate's hand, "—but Nate helped me through it all. I need to return to a normal life again. I'm going to do whatever it takes to get there."

Ryan said, "So I'd like to share with everyone what the police department has discovered in our investigation."

Silence settled over them all, and Lauren squeezed Nate's hand. He was surprised but pleased she was willing to show that small bit of affection in front of her parents. Lauren had done something for him—she made him want to be a better person. A more emotionally open person. And to face his own fears like she'd so bravely faced hers.

"Our guess is that a fraternity was responsible for both the fire at your rental and the attack at the library," Ryan said, pacing a little as he spoke. "Proximity and motive are the primary reasons for our suspicions. If we were looking at a person acting alone, we'd have trouble pinpointing the perp from all the men connected to the women who've come to your support group, but seven men together? Most abusers don't talk to others about their habits, so the entire scenario screams of a fraternity. People are much bolder as a group. They feel stronger. Of course, they're absolutely wrong. Acting as a group weakens them, and hopefully it will help us catch these men.

"Based on that information, we're focusing on two fraternities: Gamma Delta and Chi Theta. We searched their houses and both of them had the same propellant that was used to burn down your rental. All members denied any knowledge of either attack, but without any prompting from me, which tells us they knew something. However, we still have no prints or witnesses, so we have to continue the investigation."

Nate noticed the hope in Lauren's eyes. She thought the bastards who did this to her were about to be caught, but something told him they weren't there yet. He was quite sure Ryan's news would not be what they wanted to hear.

Ryan cleared his throat, glanced at his father, then continued. "There's only one problem."

"What is it?" Lorraine asked.

"We don't have any concrete evidence, only suspicions. We had someone look at Lauren's photos more closely, but there's nothing there we can use."

Lauren deflated almost immediately.

"What evidence do you need?" the elder Ryan asked.

"A witness."

Dead silence followed. No one glanced at Lauren except for Ryan.

Lauren stared at her hands and said, "I can't identify anyone, Ryan. I never saw the man who broke my window, and the others all wore masks."

Ryan nodded. "I know that, and I understand. We're hoping as time passes, something will jar your memory—a tattoo, a voice, a comment one of them made, anything."

Nate squeezed her hand and said, "If not, we'll find another way."

The look she gave him broke his heart.

He'd find the bastards if he had to do it alone.

☾

After Ryan, Cait, and Nate left, and her mother and stepfather went up to their room, Lauren lingered on the porch, held there by a thrumming in her heart. She was staring out at the lake water, soaking in the sense of calm it always gave her, when a shooting star shot across the sky in front of her. Her gaze stayed with it, watching it transform the sky from something usual to something stunning, the tail of the star lighting up the lake. Her entire countenance changed from one of fear and worry to one of delight.

She heard the door close, followed by the sound of approaching footsteps, so she whirled around, surprised to see Ryan there. "Did you forget something?"

Ryan smiled, "No. Believe it or not, it was the shooting star that convinced me I needed to come back inside." He gave her a sheepish look. "Cait believes in a lot of stories about angels. Different tales about heaven and why we're all here. Anyway, I've been thinking of talking to you privately, and that shooting star convinced Cait it was the right time, so here I am."

Lauren had no idea what this was about, but she sat down in a nearby chair, motioning for him to speak.

Ryan seemed to struggle with what he wanted to say—she could see it in his eyes and in the way he held himself. He'd spent all his adult life as a soldier or policeman, and he knew how to intimidate someone with a single glance. But there was a softer and more vulnerable side to her dear stepbrother, and he was showing it to her now. "You know I have issues with PTSD and that I had a difficult time accepting Cait into my life because of it."

She nodded, doing her best to keep her eyes from misting. Ryan had come back from the war in Iraq an amputee—something people rarely noticed now given how agile he was on his prosthetic leg—haunted by the death of his best friend. For a long time, he'd struggled for happiness, but Cait had helped him heal.

He took a seat next to her. "Don't push him away. I'm convinced you have PTSD as much as I do. How could you not after all the attacks? I know what it's like to feel like you're not good enough for someone, that you'll be a burden to that person. It's not true."

He stammered a few more times, but then said, "Nate Patterson is a good man. He has his own issues, but he's honorable. He'll respect you.

"I know you didn't ask my advice, but I'm going to give it anyway. Cait is the best thing that's ever happened to me, and every day I wake up grateful that she's next to me. Yes, I still suffer from PTSD, but she helps me through it. And the more I'm with her, the fewer episodes I have. I guess I wanted to say to give him a chance. What he helped you to do tonight was amazing."

"Thank you, Ryan. I'm glad you came back to talk to me. You're right…I do feel like a burden to the people I care about." They both stood up, and she wrapped her arms around him. "He is a good man, and he's very patient with me."

"Good. I'm glad to hear it. You need to keep telling yourself that you deserve love, Lauren, because it's the truth." He gave her a kiss and stepped away, disappearing with a final wave.

He was right. She *did* deserve love.

If she could just remember something about the bastards to put them away, she could put all this behind her and focus on Nate.

☾

Lauren couldn't fall asleep. She lay in her bed, trying to force memories that weren't there. There had to be a clue, something she'd missed. She'd closed her eyes and relived the scenario at the library multiple times, but nothing came back to her.

Nothing.

She climbed out of bed and grabbed a robe. Many times when she was upset or depressed, she'd walk down to the lake and let the waters perform their soothing magic on her soul. She crept out the back door, taking the time to close it quietly so as not to awaken her mother. She knew how upset her mom was about everything that had happened. How she hated being the cause of so much pain…

She tightened the belt on her robe and took less than ten steps before she stopped, a cool breeze washing over her, inviting her to lift her chin and tip her head back to soak in the light of the moon. The stars danced across the dark blue expanse of ethereal beauty.

At first she wasn't sure why she'd stopped—the lake always comforted her—but she realized that she hoped for a different kind of comfort tonight. She wanted to be with Nate.

She pivoted and returned to the house, changing her clothes and crafting a quick note for her mother so as not to worry. Then she retrieved her phone and took a deep breath before she punched the keys, sending a message to Nate.

Are you up?

It was almost one o'clock in the morning, but it was only a matter of seconds before he answered.

Yep.

She found her keys and sent another text as she headed toward her vehicle.

I'm in my car. Can I meet you at your place?

Sure.

He gave her his address so she punched in into her phone. About ten minutes later, she pulled into his driveway and waited. She didn't want to knock on the door for fear of awakening his brothers.

He stepped onto his front porch and made his way to the passenger side of her car, climbing in next to her. To her surprise, he leaned over and kissed her, a soft kiss that almost caused her to moan with pleasure, but she contained herself. She'd come here for a reason.

He ended the kiss and said, "You can't sleep either?"

She turned the engine off, leaving her window rolled halfway down to let in the cool, refreshing night air, and folded her hands in her lap. "No. I keep trying to recall something about the attacks. A lead to help Ryan and the cops. There must be some clue that I've overlooked. Do you have any suggestions?"

"No." He reached over for her hand. "I'd hoped visiting the spot where it happened would bring something back, but maybe it's too soon. These things take time. I'm always surprised at the details I'll remember about a working fire several weeks after it happened. My guess is it has something with that whole adrenaline, fight-or-flight instinct. You can't remember everything because you were too focused on saving yourself."

"I have a thought, but I'd like your input."

"Go ahead."

"I'd like to visit the frat houses." She gazed at him, waiting to see how he'd respond. It had occurred to her—just as it had no doubt occurred to Ryan and Nate—that the guys from the boat had been involved in the attack. Maybe it would jog her memory if she spent time around them. Maybe their voices, scent, or something else, would help bring the moment back with more clarity.

"Not alone..."

"No. I'm asking you if you'd go with me."

Nate sighed, and she hoped it wasn't because he planned on turning her down. But then he took her by surprise, nodding slowly and rubbing his thumb across the skin on the back of her hand. "I'll go with you. I don't think it will hurt, but I'll give you a fair warning that Thursday is a common party night. They may all be drunk or stoned."

"Couldn't we question them? Get Dom or Trevor to talk? Or the other one?"

"Randy? We can try. But if we're going to do it, let's go now. I don't want to go any later than this."

He opened the door to get out.

"I can drive," she said before he got out.

"I don't doubt that for a moment, but what if being that close to them upsets you, or they follow us? Are you prepared to drive under those conditions? I'd rather you keep your car here. They, whoever they are, know your vehicle. This is the one you drove when you were attacked."

"All right." She was glad she'd pulled to one side of the driveway so he could get his truck around her.

Always the gentleman, he came over to her side and opened her door. She followed him to his vehicle, but just before he held the door open for her, he spun around and cupped her face. "I know how badly you want this to work, but please promise me you won't do anything foolish. We will definitely be outnumbered, and chances are they'll be drunk."

"I promise." She had no doubt that he was right. "I appreciate you for doing this for me."

His thumb brushed her bottom lip and he leaned down, feathering her lips with a soft kiss before he dipped in for more, slanting his mouth over hers. She parted her lips for him and he groaned, just the slightest bit, but the sound made her feel very special. She touched her tongue to his and everything else fell away from her. She allowed herself to be carried away from all the negative events in her life and to just focus on him, Nate Patterson, her protector, her warrior.

When he ended the kiss, she was so caught up in him that she actually stumbled. He righted her and opened the door with a grin. Once she was settled, he leaned over and whispered in her ear, "My feelings exactly."

He closed the door and moved behind the truck, and she was glad.

She didn't want him to see her blush.

❧

Nate had conflicting feelings about what they were about to do. He'd pledged to help her, but were they making a mistake? He held her hand and kept her close as they strode down Fraternity Row in the college complex.

The two frats in question were at the far end of the Row. It wasn't hard to determine that this was a party night for many of the Greeks on campus. If he remembered correctly, there were three fraternities and four sororities.

He stopped in front of the Gamma Delta house, wanting to verify that she wished to proceed before he headed inside. One glance at her was enough to assure him of her determination. She gave him a nearly imperceptible nod, so they climbed up the staircase to the old colonial, painted in green with the Greek letters of Gamma Delta on a flag hanging from an upstairs balcony. It was made of clapboard with some brick, but the old building had fallen into disrepair. The grounds were not well kept either.

The door flew open and two men stumbled out. They did a double take before continuing down the staircase as if they hadn't seen them.

"Should we knock?" she whispered.

"No," he replied. "Let's see what they're doing. I doubt they'd hear the knock anyway. The music is pretty loud."

She squeezed his hand in a death grip as he opened the door and led the way into a large foyer full of college students, the smell of beer permeating the area.

Nate took in the high ratio of men to women. One woman sat in the corner, barely alert, and another sat at a bar stool in the back, surrounded by three men encouraging her to drink. She didn't look willing. He decided to make that his first stop.

Once they reached her side, he noticed one of the men harassing her was Randy Brooks. He held a tight grip on the woman's arm as she tried to pull away. Nate grabbed his wrist and said, "Let her go."

As soon as Randy released her, the trembling girl took off toward the door running. Randy spun on his heel with his fist pulled back, ready to lash out at the offender. He missed his target because Nate grabbed his fist, twisting it hard enough to drop him to his knees.

"You son of a bitch. I was going to have her tonight." After he fell to his knees, he took the time to glance up at his attacker. "Who the hell are you?" His words slurred to the point that Nate was pretty sure he'd topple backward from a mere touch.

Then his gaze caught sight of Lauren. "Never mind. I'll take her instead."

For a moment, Lauren's fear took over. Standing in a room full of drunken men threatened to send her into a full-scale panic attack, but she forced herself to keep her gaze on Nate. He would never let anything bad happened to her. She knew that down to her bones.

Then something strange happened. She wasn't just afraid anymore—she was just pissed. Randy had openly admitted that he was pumping a woman full of booze in the hopes of having sex with her later, probably so she wouldn't be able to fight or get away.

"Like hell you will. You'll never touch her." Nate grabbed him by the neck and tossed him back so he lay prone on the floor. He hadn't meant to throw him that far, but the thought of the piece of shit touching Lauren didn't exactly sit well. The guy's eyes closed in a drunken stupor, or so Nate guessed since the jackass hadn't landed that hard.

"What the hell are you doing here, Patterson?" Dominic's voice came from behind him.

The men in the room who were sober enough to listen all stopped their conversations, picking up on Dom's tone. "And why is *she* here?"

When he stopped in front of them, he smiled at Lauren. A sick grin that made Nate want to punch him in the face. "Well, well, if it isn't Lauren Grant. Have you decided to join our group? We'd be happy to make you a special member. You'd only have to pass a few tests."

Nate balled his fists and did his best to maintain control. "We're just visiting. Thought we'd see what Gamma Delta was all about. You say you're innocent, yet the last woman ran out of here as soon as Randy Brooks let go of her."

"We don't force anyone to stay here. They're here of their own free will. We had a keg party tonight. Anyone is welcome, which is the only reason I haven't tossed you out on your ass, Patterson."

Dominic wasn't that big. He was tall but flabby. Out of shape. Nate chuckled. "You and who else? You certainly couldn't do it on your own, Miller."

Dominic laughed, a boisterous forced laugh that made Lauren step closer to Nate, and he wondered if it had triggered a memory for her. Several other frat brothers joined Dom, all laughing and converging on them.

"Nate, let's go." She whispered against his chest so the others couldn't hear her.

He would be happy to oblige her, but not until he set things straight with these cocky bastards. Nate wasn't afraid of Dominic Miller. He was the type of coward who made others do his dirty work. All mouth and no action. But after glancing into Lauren's frightened eyes one last time, he decided he didn't want to risk upsetting her. He glanced around and noticed she was now the only female in the room. The few others had apparently taken off during their conversation.

Nate said, "If I didn't have the lady with me, I'd take you on, Miller. You aren't man enough to do any damage, but I'm taking her away. I'll find you another time."

He put his hand on the small of her back and motioned her toward the door, but a meaty hand grasped his shoulder. "Like hell you're leaving," Dom said. "You're staying. You need to be taught a lesson, and I'll watch your woman for you." He reached for Lauren, but that was the wrong thing to do.

CHAPTER ELEVEN

NATE SPUN AROUND AND LANDED a fist in Dom's face, then grabbed him by the throat, but not before Dom managed to yell, "Take care of him!"

Four guys grabbed him from behind as he sent Dom flying, so he shoved Lauren toward the door. "Go. I'll catch you." He picked one fool up and tossed him to the side and stopped another weak fist that jabbed at him ineffectually. He was about to go for a fourth when a loud voice interrupted them from the staircase at the far end of the room.

"Leave him be!"

The brothers all backed away, and Dominic picked himself off the floor, rubbing his jaw.

Trevor Hutton came down the stairs. "Dom, let them go. We don't need any more trouble." The guy looked a little old for the activities going on inside the frat. Hadn't someone said he'd already graduated?

Dom said, "I was just inviting the Grant woman to stay for a while, that's all. I meant them no harm."

"Get the hell out of here, Patterson, and take her with you. Neither of you are welcome here."

Nate moved over to Lauren's side and ushered her out the door with a parting comment. "Some hospitality you offer."

Once they were off away from the dorms, he tugged Lauren to a stop with his hand. "Are you all right?"

She nodded, tears in her eyes. "I just want to go. I don't want to ever step foot in there again. This was wrong, so wrong."

"Did you remember anything? Did anyone look familiar?"

"No. No memories, nothing, just a burning desire to get away before they hurt you." She pulled on him and they resumed their path back to his truck.

Once they arrived, she headed for the passenger side of his vehicle, but she stopped suddenly and spun around. "Please don't ever do that again." A tear escaped down one cheek.

He cupped her face and whispered, "Lauren, I could have handled them. They were all drunk, unsteady on their feet. Doesn't matter that there were more of them. They weren't a challenge."

"But I don't want you hurt because of me. It didn't help. I'll have to find another way. But I will figure this out, no matter how long it takes me." She grabbed his shirt and yanked him toward her, kissing him hard on the lips, devouring him with a passion that surprised him.

It also had him hard in an instant. She wouldn't let go of him.

Nate glanced around. The area was devoid of any activity, but he still felt a little unsettled about where they were. "I'm getting you away from here first."

Once they were off the campus, he said, "I want you more than I've ever wanted anyone, Lauren, but I don't know what to do. I...I don't want to push you too far."

"Just find a hidden spot to park and kiss me."

Surprised at her boldness, he stepped on the gas. "We aren't that far from my house." He headed home, grateful for all the green traffic lights. She kept caressing him with her hands—running her fingers up his arm to grip his bicep, or feeling his chest—in a seductive way that almost had him stopping in the middle of the street.

He finally pulled into his own driveway, shut the vehicle off, and turned to kiss her, ravaging her mouth, twining his tongue with hers until they were both breathless. He mumbled, "This isn't going to work for me." He climbed out and moved to the other side to open the car door. Though he'd planned to take her to his room, she pulled him up toward her. He joined her in the truck and lifted her onto his lap so she was straddling him. Her lips found his again and she leaned into him, pressing her breasts against him so firmly he could actually feel her nipples peak through the material of her shirt.

To his surprise, she took his hands and put them at her waist, lifting her shirt and guiding him inside. "Touch me, please."

Nate didn't wait for another invitation. After reaching around to unhook her bra, he scooped his hands under the thin material in the front so he could cup her breasts. He groaned as her soft skin filled his rough hands, and he did his best to be gentle, bringing his thumbs up to her nipples, rubbing the tips lightly until she moaned in the back of her throat, a sweet sound that went straight to his dick, making him even harder if that were possible.

"Lauren, you're so beautiful." Her breasts were perfect, just perfect. Not too big, but enough to fill his hands and a little more. He rained kisses down her neck, but she froze, so he stopped, bringing his gaze up to meet hers.

"Lauren, is something wrong?" The fear in her eyes made him drop his hands.

"Please stop. I'm sorry, but stop." She struggled against him, but there was no place for her to go.

He stilled her hands and said, "Look at me, Lauren. This is Nate, I'm not going to hurt you. I won't do anything you don't want me to do, but let me help you readjust."

Tears streamed down her face, and they were close enough to the garage light that he could see the fear vanish from her gaze, replaced by confusion. She peered at him and nodded.

"I'm going to reach behind you and hook your bra. Do you want to position it so it's comfortable?"

She nodded, her eyes still darting back and forth, but she did as he suggested. She started to move off of him, and he said, "Could I please guide you? We're kind of in tight quarters here, and I'm in a difficult position." His erection, while it had started to shrink, was directly in the path of her knee.

She closed her eyes and mumbled, "Sorry. Show me which way is best."

He managed, with quite a bit of squirming and maneuvering, to get her turned around on his lap so she faced the passenger door. She pushed on the door, but he didn't want to end things this way.

He placed his lips against the side of her forehead and whispered, "Talk to me. Please? Was it something I did? I need to know so I won't do it again."

Lauren relaxed against him. This was Nate, not some attacker or a rapist.

Nate.

She sighed and gripped his arms as she fell back against his chest, resting her head on his shoulder. "Forgive me. I know you'd never hurt me. It's just..."

"Take your time."

His quiet strength and patience soothed her. She needed Nate in her life. Why had she struggled against the thought? "I can't explain it. Something popped into my mind, and it brought up a memory of the attack at the library."

"Something in particular that I did?"

"No." She thought for a moment, trying to recall if there had been a definite trigger. "No, I was enjoying us...you...your touch. I...I felt things I haven't felt in a long time. I'm sorry, Nate. I can't explain how my mind works. I'm not sure what to say."

"If you don't feel up to driving, I can bring you home. Whatever you prefer."

"Would my car be in your way if I leave it here?"

"No. I have to work tomorrow, but I can bring it back this weekend."

"I'll have Mallory bring me over to get it tomorrow. Thank you for going with me, for being my protector." She sat up enough to kiss him lightly on the lips. "Why don't you take me home?"

They traveled in silence, but when he pulled into her driveway, he said, "I do want to continue this with you. I hope I didn't frighten you away for good. We can figure this out together. Call me Saturday or Sunday and let me know if there's anything else I can help you with. In fact, I'd love to take you out to dinner Saturday night."

She nodded, unable to say what was in her heart. Truth was, she wanted this relationship to work so badly that she hated herself for shutting down on him. It would wreak havoc on her heart if she lost her chance with him. And yet...she was so embarrassed, so angry at herself, she wasn't sure she could face him again. "I'll call you," she said, not sure that she meant it.

He gave her a quick kiss, and she closed the door, waving at him.

Nate arrived at work Sunday morning just in time to hear the alarm go off. The dispatcher informed them that it was a car accident with a spill.

He grabbed his gear, silently grateful for a task to keep his mind off Lauren and the fact that she hadn't called him to go out to dinner. He'd texted her once that morning, but she had begged off, saying she was tired. If she felt better later, she'd said, she'd call him back, but he hadn't heard a thing. His mother would have likely told him it was his fault because it was the man's job to invite someone out for a date, but Lauren was so fragile that he didn't want to push her. He may have gone too far the other night.

That one thought niggled at him over and over again.

He climbed into the EMT vehicle, trying to assure himself that there were plenty of other available women if this thing with Lauren didn't work out.

It didn't help. He wanted Lauren. At first he'd thought his interest in her might be tied up in his desire to protect her, but things had become very clear to him the other night. Lauren was special, and the way he felt about her was special, too.

As soon as Sam climbed in next to him, he put the vehicle in gear and stepped on the gas. Siren blaring, he focused on the road and listened as the dispatcher gave them more information.

"Female driver pinned in the vehicle. Car on its side with gas leaking. No other victims noted. ETA?"

Sam replied, "Three minutes." He gave their vehicle number. "What kind of vehicle?"

"Chevy SUV is the only report."

Sam let out a slow whistle and shot him a sidelong look. "Now don't go wild on the scene just because the car is similar to Mom's."

"I'll keep it under control, but we'll get her out." Adrenaline flooded him. Yes, he'd get her out if it killed him. Not only was it his job—it was the one thing he could do, again and again, to try and make up for the fact that he'd failed to save his own mother.

"We won't have much time if there's a leak. We'll have to work quickly to avoid a fire."

"I know, but we should have enough time to get her out. She's probably unconscious, hit her head on the steering wheel or something. She could be awake by the time we arrive."

"Airbag wouldn't knock her unconscious."

They arrived on the scene and noticed two other civilian vehicles pulled in close. One woman was frantically using her phone while a man was crouched at the door of the vehicle, apparently doing his best to extricate the trapped victim.

He made a silent gesture to Sam, requesting that he speak to the two witnesses. Nate couldn't…he wouldn't be able to register anything they had to say. His focus was on that car, so similar to their mother's…

Visions of that day bounced in his head, resurfacing as he approached the vehicle with confidence he didn't feel. The memories took him over…

She skidded on a rainy day and hit the side of a bridge. Their car had been mangled after hitting the bridge in several places before coming to rest in a nearby ditch. He was in the back seat because he'd injured his leg during baseball practice, and he couldn't open his door or unlock his seat belt.

His mother—Lord, his dear mother—had hit her head on the driver door and blood was everywhere. She kept screaming for Nate to get out, to free himself and not worry about her, but he ignored her.

"Mom, I'll get you out. Don't worry."

"Nate, the car could go up in flames. I smell gas. Get out. You have to get out. Your father couldn't handle losing both of us. You have to be there for your brothers. Please just listen to me and get out."

Her voice sounded weak and thready, and he renewed his struggle with his seat belt. Sirens could be heard in the distance, but they couldn't get there fast enough to save his mother.

He finally freed himself and leaned over the back of the seat, only to freeze. His mother's breathing had changed, and she panted like a dog. "Nate. I love you. Tell your brothers I love them. I'm so sorry. I tried…to stop…to turn the wheel…I couldn't." Every breath was a struggle for her.

"Mom, it's all right. I'll get you out." But somehow he knew he wouldn't. He was eighteen at the time, scrawny, no muscle definition. The steering wheel had her pinned, crushing her against the seat. He pushed and pushed, but it never budged, so he climbed out to try to wrench it free from the outside.

He yanked on her door until it came open. "Mom, I got it. Mom, I'll get you free, you'll see." He grabbed her arm and tugged.

"Nate..." her eyes glazed over as she spoke to him. Her one free hand reached for him. Her eyes closed and he yelled at her. "Mom, no! Mom, stay awake. Stay with me."

He pushed and shoved and tugged for all he was worth until a brawny set of arms lifted him and set him away from his mother.

Two firefighters struggled to pull her out, one yelling, "We need the jaws."

But the second one shook his head, whispering to the first. "It's not worth it. Her chest is crushed. Even if we got her out now, she'll never make it."

Nate watched the man feel her pulse in two different places before he shook his head at his partner. The second one turned toward him and said, "Sorry, kid. There's nothing we can do."

Nate had screamed and screamed and screamed, finally resting his head on top of hers until his father arrived and pulled him off.

That one moment had made him want to be the best possible firefighter and EMT, so he could help every victim possible. He'd sworn to never again allow his emotions to slow down his reaction time.

It was the only way.

Nate pinched himself, needing to reorient to the present moment. He desperately needed to save this victim because he'd failed to save his mother. Sam checked the outside of the ruined vehicle while he climbed up on the door since the car was on its side, driver door up. He glanced in at the woman and saw exactly what he'd expected. She was unconscious, a deflated airbag hanging down the front of her body. He reached for her hand and tugged on it, "Ma'am, wake up. Please, I need your help."

Nothing.

"What do you see?" Sam shouted. "Can we get her out? There's quite a bit of gas collecting behind the car." The fire trucks had arrived and were beginning to deal with the spill. His captain arrived, assessed the situation, and barked out orders.

"Patterson? What do you need?"

"I think I can get her out if I cut the seat belt." He opened the car door carefully as he braced himself across the twisted metal.

Sam found the right tool and handed it to him as he climbed up next to Nate, the car making a strange squealing sound beneath them.

Captain yelled, "I want five men on the other side of the car holding it up. I don't want it toppling."

Nate cut the belt and Sam reached for one shoulder to keep the driver from falling down. "Hold her, Sam. Don't let her go." He tossed the tool down and reached for her waist.

As soon as he touched the woman, her eyes flew open. "What, where, oh no…" Her eyes closed again.

"Stay with me, Ma'am. What's your name?" He changed his position and reached down to wrest her legs out while Sam held her shoulders in place.

"Betty Worthington. Ow." He felt a bump on her leg, probably a fracture.

"I'm sorry, but this might hurt a bit."

"Just get me out. Please. I don't want to die. I have grandchildren."

Nate continued the conversation, knowing how important it was to keep her alert. "You do? How many? Tell me all about them."

She spoke softly to him for a moment, telling him about her little granddaughter, and he finally managed to free her. At his request, she reached for his shoulder, and he lifted her slowly out of the car with an assist from Sam. "Thank you for saving me," she said. "You firemen are not appreciated enough. Thank you so much. Ow…ignore me, just keep going."

Moments later, they lowered her onto a gurney next to the car.

Her parting words were, "Bless you two boys. Bless you."

Nate smiled and nodded to her, soaking in the look of gratitude in her eyes. "Doing our job, Ms. Worthington."

Relief swelled through his body as she was carted away from them. Sam patted his shoulder and said, "Well done."

"Nice job, Patterson," the chief said, giving him a pointed look.

He'd connected with a survivor *and* he'd helped her. At that moment, he made a vow to himself. He wouldn't step away from Lauren unless she truly wanted him gone.

Though he'd never admit it to anyone, he often felt his mother's presence—her influence. She'd been with him today, no question, and her message had come across clearly: Lauren Grant needed him…and he needed Lauren Grant.

CHAPTER TWELVE

LAUREN FELT A BIT GUILTY. She'd told Nate she would call him on Saturday, but Saturday had come and gone and she hadn't reached out to him at all other than their short text exchange. Though her feelings for him were stronger than ever, she was confused and overwhelmed. She'd hoped everything would become clearer to her if she took some time for herself.

Clarity eluded her.

Nothing had come from their trip to the frat house.

Nothing.

Where did she go from here? She sat on her bed and pulled her chart out from its hiding place, spreading it out across the coverlet so she could study it. The answer was here, she was certain. Every attack and near attack that had been brought to her attention had been carefully documented. She had the intelligence to analyze it, but was she too emotionally connected to the problem?

Fingering the chart, she chewed on her lip. Maybe she needed someone else's opinion. She understood how working with someone else could lead to a breakthrough. Was it time to share it with someone else?

Yes, she needed to, but with whom?

Ryan or Jake were obvious answers, but they would violate her confidentiality agreement with the victims. If word got out that she had gone to the police with the information, people would stop coming to her for help. She needed them to know she would never invade their privacy.

The other issue was that she'd lose control of the document, and she hadn't copied all of the details over to the flash drive. The answer was here, she was certain of it. Yet no matter how long she stared at it, she couldn't pull all the threads together.

She'd like to show it to Nate, despite the awkwardness of their missed date, but something told her he'd make her turn it over to Ryan. Again, not a possibility she was ready to entertain.

Caitlyn? No, she'd feel compelled to share it with her husband.

Mallory?

Her mother?

Her stepfather?

Everyone who came to mind she was certain would convince her to give the document to the police, which was not an option at this point. She rested her head on her arms, surprised at how sleepy she was since it was only mid-afternoon.

No matter. It was a Sunday, so she yawned and closed her eyes, just for a few moments.

As she drifted off to sleep, she thought of what Ryan had said about Caitlyn believing in angels and a fanciful idea formed in her mind. If only guardian angels were real, and someone who'd moved on to the other side could help her.

How she wished such angels existed.

If they did, she'd call for their help.

☾

A peacefulness came over Lauren unlike any she'd ever felt before. She had no fear, no worries, only curiosity. The colors around her were magnificent, and as she twirled around to take in her surroundings, they washed over her body, warming her insides and making her giggle with giddiness.

"I like that. 'Tis much better to see you happy," a female voice called out to her.

Lauren came to an abrupt halt and searched out the voice, her gaze falling on a lovely woman. The colors she'd been enjoying fell away to reveal a royal chamber, the likes of which she'd never seen before other than in drawings of the Scottish castles of old.

"We agreed 'twould be best for me to deliver our message."

"We?"

"Aye, your ancestors, your angels. You called for us. Aye, you opened your heart and asked for help from your angels." The woman had long blonde hair and blue eyes, and the aura of kindness that surrounded her made Lauren want to move closer and settle her head on her shoulder.

She started to move toward her, but then took a step back when the woman said, "You may, if you like."

"I may?"

The woman laughed. "Put your head on my shoulder. Your thoughts are strong enough for me to hear them sometimes. You have earned the comfort you yearn for."

How was it possible that this stranger could read her mind?

Lauren shook her head, not knowing what to say. Was this a dream, or was she really here?

The woman took two steps toward her, her hands folded in front of her. "I don't have much time. I have two things to tell you. They are both important. The first is that you must give that chart to Ryan."

Lauren stared at the woman, unable to believe the words she'd just uttered. "What chart?"

"The chart you've so carefully crafted. I know you wish to keep it, but unfortunately you cannot see it. You need the help of another. Relinquish it to Ryan."

"I can't…" she whispered as she took a step back, unable to believe they were discussing something she'd revealed to no one. She'd never told anyone about her chart. It had been her secret. And how did this woman know about Ryan?

"Mayhap not yet, but you will be ready soon. 'Tis time to move forward with your life, my dear. Your burdens have been very heavy, but we are here to help you, guide you, so to speak."

"You speak with a Gaelic accent. What time period are you from?" Her heartbeat sped up. "I would love to know more about it."

"Child, I do not have the time to tell you about the Grants in medieval Scotland. Continue your research and you'll find out all you wish to know. I have only a few moments to speak with you, and there are far more important topics for us to discuss."

"You said there are two things you need to tell me…"

"I did, did I not? The other you are not ready for yet, but I'll tell you anyway. You may not give me the opportunity to visit you again."

"The second thing?" Something told her it was important, and she felt compelled to push the woman.

"Aye." She paused before she spoke, holding her outstretched hands flat, palms up. "Nate is your Alex."

"My Alex? What does that mean?"

"It means that Nate has the three most important characteristics a lass could want in a partner. I'll only tell you one, though your stepbrother already spoke with you about it. Nathan is *honorable* and that is an essential part of love."

"Who are you? Please tell me so I can research your family, your descendants." Lauren had the frantic urge to grab the woman and never let go.

As if she read her mind again, she said, "Nay, my dear. 'Tis not your time yet. You have much to do." The woman smiled and blew her a kiss, fading into a vapor and disappearing from view. "You're verra fortunate that you have found your Alex. Many never do."

When Lauren awakened, she checked the clock. She's been asleep for over an hour. Rubbing the sleep from her eyes, she hopped off the bed and headed toward the bathroom, but something stopped her dead in her tracks.

Her chart. She spun around, relaxing a bit when she noticed it remained in the same place she'd left it. She frowned, her fingers reaching up to knead her forehead. Something…

A dream. That was what it had been. She'd dreamed of a beautiful blonde woman, older than she was but younger than her mother. The woman had given her two messages.

Fleeting images forced her to stop and sit in a chair, trying to recall every bit of the dream, but she could only summon bits and pieces—a beautiful woman who'd said something about ancestors and Nate being her Alex. What in blazes did it mean?

She'd also reiterated that Nate was honorable—and that it was one of the most important characteristics she could look for in a man.

Yes, that strange bit about Nate had been one of the messages, but what was the other one? No matter how she tried, she couldn't conjure up the rest of her dream.

Nate is your Alex. The words ran through her head again, persistent.

She hoped that meant something good. She fell back onto her

bed in a huff, folding her chart up and restoring it to its place in the lockbox. Nate had been wonderful on Thursday. He'd gone to that frat house with her in the middle of the night—all because she'd asked him. And he'd protected her and treated her like she was precious to him.

He'd also given her the best kiss she'd ever experienced—a kiss that had almost made her forget her past for a few moments. A tear slid down her cheek at the memory of how wonderful it had felt to be in his arms, to feel his hands on her skin—to *feel*.

Then she'd pushed him away, and he'd been wonderful about that, too. She moved over to the window, noticing her car in the driveway. Ultimately, she'd asked her mother and stepfather to retrieve it for her, not wanting to answer the dozens of questions Mallory would inevitably ask. Her mother hadn't commented on the strangeness of the situation. She'd just looked at her with hope in her eyes.

Hope that Lauren felt, too.

She picked her phone up and punched in a text to Nate.

Sorry. I should have called.

He answered quickly. **Not on a call, but working.**

Maybe another night?

Absolutely.

She thought hard before she punched in the next thought.

Don't give up on me?

Never.

Have to go to the library.

Be careful.

Still daylight.

Meet someone?

I'll try my friend Stacy. Talk later?

Yes.

She texted Stacy, surprised to discover her friend was already on her way to the library. She lived closer to Cornell, but she did have family nearby and often went to the library. She was also working on an advanced degree.

Lauren, are you all right? Haven't heard from you in a while. I've been worried.

Yes. Difficult times. I'll fill you in.

I've missed you. If you ever need anything...

I know.

She regretted hiding from her friends the way she had. It was time to engage with life again and stop hiding. *One step at a time. Stacy, first. She understood exactly what she'd been through.*

They made arrangements to meet at a row in the parking lot, so she grabbed her books and threw them in her bag, not wanting to miss her. She made a quick explanation to her mom so she wouldn't worry, then rushed out of the house.

Almost to her car, she nearly dropped her bag when another thought popped in her mind.

Gaelic.

The woman had spoken in a Gaelic accent and mentioned the Grants in medieval Scotland. Now she had a new reason to throw herself into research about Clan Grant. All the way to the library, she thought about her research on Scottish history in the 1200s, specifically around the time of the Battle of Largs, but she couldn't recall anything about an Alex. Or an Alexander maybe? She pulled into the parking lot, pleased to see Stacy waiting for her as promised.

As soon as she locked her car, Stacy strode over to her and wrapped her arms around her. "I'm so sorry you were hurt, Lauren. Anytime you want to talk about it, punch a pillow, whatever, I'm here."

Lauren said, "I'm okay. Thanks for waiting for me. How long will you be here?"

"Probably an hour or two." As they walked toward the entrance together, Stacy said, "I'll text you when I'm ready to leave, or you can let me know when you're ready. Were you able to use any of the moves we learned in self-defense class?"

"I did. But it didn't do much against seven men."

"I'm so sorry." She stopped and rubbed her friend's arm. "I can't imagine how terrifying that must have been for you. Seven…wow. I hope your stepbrothers find those assholes. Just text me when you're ready. I can walk you out to your car even if I'm staying."

"Thanks, Stacy. It means a lot." They moved toward the library again, and Lauren was glad. She didn't want to fall apart in public. Once they were inside, they split up and Lauren climbed the stairs to the history section. Her favorite table was empty, so she settled her things before she moved through the many tomes, her fingers lightly caressing the spines of some of her favorite books. When she located the two she needed, she brought them back to the table and opened one, checking the table of contents for the sections on The Battle of Largs.

It didn't take long for her to become immersed in the now-familiar saga. The Norse raiders. The Scots' last stand...

An hour later, she bolted out of her chair without thinking about her surroundings. A few people stared at her, so she took a few deep breaths and settled back in her chair.

There in front of her was the answer to her question. She'd thought her dream had been about Clan Grant only because it was her family's surname, but the connection was deeper than expected. Pulling her phone out, she took a picture of the section she'd just read in the old book.

"Most accounts of the battle claim the turning point was when the chieftain of Clan Grant rode onto the beach in a gold helm atop his mail-clad destrier. The tales agree that Alexander Grant swung his sword with a fury the Norse had never seen before, sending many of them racing back to their galley ship. Grant had two brothers, Robert and Brodie, who fought by his side. The Grant brothers had trained one of the most formidable and skilled army of warriors ever seen. In fact, many attribute the victory of the Scots to the fighting skills of Clan Grant. They were mightiest with their swords."

Lauren read the section two more times before she rested her head down on the desk, pushing the book aside. What did it all mean? She closed her eyes for just a moment, wishing the woman would come back to explain everything.

But when she drifted into a state between wakefulness and sleep, someone else appeared in her mind's eye. A young boy of about ten jumped out from behind a tree in a forest of old-growth trees and said, "Dinnae forget my slinger! I took care of those pignuts."

She jerked back up, her eyes flying open, though at least no one seemed to notice her this time. Was all the stress causing her to lose control?

She leaned back in her chair, crossing her arms to slow the shivers now coursing through her body. Alex Grant was the great chieftain of Clan Grant...her Gaelic ancestors, if she believed in such a thing, wanted her to know that Nate was her Alex.

The thoughts were so overwhelming, she didn't even notice Stacy's approach until her friend took the seat across from her.

She whispered, "Lauren, you look like you did that time we went to the haunted house during your junior year. Are you all right?"

Lauren pulled herself out of her historical stupor so she could respond to her friend. "I'm fine. Some things in history are so interesting. I was just reading about the Battle of Largs."

Stacy gave her a puzzling look. "Never heard of it."

"I know. Maybe that's why I find it so interesting. It's pretty obscure."

"Sooo...I've been thinking about something for a while. I just moved into a new apartment, and I have a spare bedroom. Would you be interested in rooming with me again? It's in downtown Summerhill, not Ithaca, but it's on the south end of town, so it would be closer to the university than your house on the lake. The rent is pretty reasonable, but I could use some help with the bills. Besides, it would be fun to have you around."

Lauren perked up, surprised by the offer. She and Stacy had been good friends since they were undergrads. They'd even shared a dorm room for two years. Now Stacy was getting her masters' degree in social work at Summerhill, while she continued working at the Center. "That sounds great. If you're serious, I might be interested. When would you like me to move in?"

"Anytime. I don't have any classes tomorrow morning. Why don't you stop over and take a look then?"

"I'd love to, and thanks for the offer. I think it's just what I need. Living at home has been fine, but I'm ready for something different."

Her life had just taken a turn for the better.

CHAPTER THIRTEEN

TWO NIGHTS LATER, LAUREN SAT in Nate's truck after dinner with him at the restaurant at the local winery. The venue had been his idea—and the new experience had delighted her.

"Your food was good?" he asked as he backed out of the lot.

"Yes. The salmon was done perfectly. Thank you for inviting me."

He reached for her hand as he drove, hanging on to it lightly, his thumb caressing the inside of her wrist at her pulse point. Nate did that often, she noticed, just a slow caress with his thumb. She'd never realized something so soothing could also feel sensual. The only thought that filled her mind was that Nate was her Alex. What could it mean?

"My friend Stacy met me at the library and offered me a place to stay. I don't want to keep living with my mom and Ryan Sr. I'd rather be independent again." She wondered what he would think of it. For some reason, she hadn't told him over dinner, wanting to keep their conversation light and easy, like a normal couple on a normal date.

Her mother had been hesitant to accept her plan, but Stacy's place was in a nice apartment complex. There was even a small deck off the back.

"Oh, that's nice. Where is it?"

She explained the location, and he held her hand all the while, caressing her in that same way, the warmth of his touch traveling up her arm in a tingle that she found strangely erotic. Was it because of her pulse?

"Do you need my help? I'm off on Thursday and Saturday this week."

"I don't have much left, mostly clothes and books. Most of my things were lost to the fire. I'm sure my brothers can help me."

He grinned and caught her gaze. "I'm sure they could, but they wouldn't enjoy it as much as I would. Allow me to help. Please? I know you'll deny it, but I'm guessing you're still sore. Carrying clothes and heavy books will only exhaust you."

She couldn't help but laugh. "And how do you know I'll deny it?" He was right, but she didn't want to admit that to him yet.

"Because I think you and I have a few things in common. It's not easy for you to admit when something's bothering you."

"Now, why would *we* avoid mentioning something like that?"

"Because *we* don't want to be a burden to anyone." He caught her gaze again. "I'm guessing you feel you've burdened your mom and stepfather too much. Am I right?"

She pondered his uncanny ability to sense the truth about her. He claimed it was because they were alike. Were they? She stared straight ahead when she answered. "Yes, you're right."

Honorable…that was the word the angel and her stepbrother had used to describe Nate. No description could be more appropriate. Every ounce of him screamed of respect and decency. Didn't the incident in his truck the other night say it all?

His voice lowered to a whisper. "Does that mean you'll allow me to help you?"

She peeked at him, a warmth spreading through her again as his fingers wrapped around hers. "Yes. I would appreciate it."

They'd almost arrived at her house, and she was surprised to see her mother's car was gone. In fact, no one appeared to be home. They had the place to themselves.

The woman in her dream had told her Nate was her Alex. Though it was ludicrous to believe the blonde woman had been Alexander Grant's wife, that her ancestors were actually trying to help her, she believed it nonetheless. And she knew they were right about Nate. While she wasn't ready to tell him about the dream, she did want him to be part of her future. And that meant trusting him.

"Nate," she said as he parked, "I just want you to know that I'm committed to this relationship, also. I know I act a little…well, odd at times, but I do like you. Very much. You've been so patient with me, and I hope you'll continue to be. I wish I could tell you how long it will take me to get past all this, but I don't have any idea. What I do know is that I want this. I want *us*."

"I do, too," he said, staring into her eyes. "I'm not going anywhere."

"I'd like to share something with you, but I would need you to keep it to yourself for now. I especially don't want you to share this information with my family." She chewed on the corner of her lip, hoping he'd agree. If not, where would she go next?

He gave her a thoughtful look. "I can promise that, as long as keeping quiet about it doesn't mean putting your life at risk."

She considered it for another moment before nodding. "Come inside and I'll show you."

He helped her out of his truck and walked inside with her, her heart speeding up just a little at the prospect of sharing her secret with this man, her Alex.

She unlocked the door with her key, then motioned for him to follow her up the stairs. Her bedroom was large because it was one of the original rooms before her stepfather built an addition to the house. Her double bed sat in the middle of the room. She indicated for Nate to sit on the bed, and as soon as he was settled, she retrieved the chart from the lock box. She carried it over to the bed, then unfolded the heavy paper until all eight sections were lying flat across her bed.

He glanced at the fine strokes on the heavy paper: the dates, the names, and all the details, compiled in her code. "What is this?" he asked, glancing up at her with a puzzled look.

She sat opposite him on the bed, crossing her legs, her hands folded in her lap. "Something I've worked very hard on over the past few years." She ran her hand fondly across the surface of the section closest to her. "It has everything."

Nate quirked his brow at her. "Everything?"

She pointed to the top of the document. "It starts up there."

Nate leaned over to read the first entry at the top of the chart. "Lauren Grant..." he drew out the words, tilting his head up to stare at her. "Is this what I think it is? Tell me, please, because I don't want to guess."

She could see the concern in his face, or was it fury? Fury at her, or fury or what the chart represented?

"That's the date I was raped. Each rectangle on the chart represents another attack on the campus, at least, according to a victim who came to my group or spoke to me privately. I only used the women's initials, but I documented the location, the time of day, and all the important details."

His gaze took in the rest of the document, pausing at some spots before. "Your name is on here three times," he finally said.

"It is. The first attack, the arson that burned down the house, and the attack at the library. I believe they may all be connected."

"Lauren, there are over fifty entries here."

"I know. Isn't that sad?" She again brought her fingers across the paper she'd worked so diligently on, the chronicle she hoped would convict the bastards who wanted to keep her quiet.

"I'm sure you've showed this to Ryan and Jake."

She uncrossed her legs and jumped off the bed. "No. You promised me you wouldn't tell them."

He followed her as she backed up toward the wall. He grasped her hands and cocooned them inside his. "Lauren. Listen to me. I know I promised, and I will not betray that confidence, but you have to give this to Ryan. This could solve your crime."

She shook her head, trying to pull her hands away from him. "No, no..."

"Sweetheart, don't leave me." He gathered her in his arms and whispered to her. "I won't tell him, but I want *you* to show him. I want you to realize that this could be our best chance of finding those creeps...and of preventing them from hurting any other women."

Her entire insides seemed to bubble as if she were close to bursting, close to losing every bit of her control that she fought so hard to maintain. She grabbed ahold of his shirt near the collar, clutching the fabric in her hand. "No, Nate, I can't just give this away. This would violate the trust these women put in me. It's no different than the HIPAA rules they use at the hospital. If I gave it to the police, I could risk losing the reputation I've worked so hard to build for my support group, maybe even for Stacy's Center. No one would trust me again if they found out I turned this information over to the authorities. Everything is here. I need to figure this out myself. I'm an intelligent person. I just wanted another pair of eyes to look at this with me. I was hoping you..." She pushed away from him.

"Shhh…I'll help you. Calm down. We'll figure this out."

One look at the tears on her face told him he needed to be very careful. She was close to going over the edge, and he needed to pull her back. "Lauren, listen to me. I'm here for you. I promise to help you in any way I can."

"You won't take my chart, will you? You promised." She swiped at her tears with one hand and hugged herself around the waist with the other.

"I won't take it. No. It's yours." How the hell was he going to convince her to do the right thing?

Slowly, very slowly. "Come here, sweetheart. Please? I just want to hold you. In fact, fold it up and put it away. We'll study it another day. Hide it wherever you want. I'll turn my back, and I promise not to watch where you put it."

She reached for the chart and began to fold it, so he spun around to face the wall. "Put it in a safe place, and then we'll talk."

"You're the first person I've trusted enough to look at it. I just wanted you to help me to look at it from a different point of view. That's all."

He heard her rustling, knowing she was putting it away. He didn't like having his back to her—part of him was afraid she'd bolt on him—but something told him it was important to her. "Let me know when you've put it away."

Her sniffling told him she was still in the room. "I promise to help you through this, no matter what. You believe me, don't you?" He had to convince her. He may have failed to save his own mother, but he could be there for Lauren. He could help her. He loved her.

What? Where the hell had that come from? The thought rocked him to his core. His break up with Mandy had convinced him that he wasn't any good at love. That maybe he was too damaged for it.

But he was falling for Lauren.

"There. I put it away. Let's never mention it again." She stood in front of her desk, looking so small he wanted to wrap his arms around her forever.

"Sit with me? Can we just talk?" He sat back on the bed, holding his arms open for her, hoping she'd come to him.

Lauren stared at the floor, another tear escaping one eye before she took a hesitant step toward him. Before he knew it, she'd settled onto his lap. She wrapped her hands around his back, holding him close, and buried her face in his shoulder as a gauntlet of pain erupted from her soul, tears drenching his shirt.

And he held her. He held her, rubbing her back, whispering to her, anything he could to keep her with him.

When her crying changed to sniffles, she tipped her face toward his neck. He could feel her warm breath coming in spasms. "I'm sorry."

"Don't be. You've done nothing wrong."

"I don't know what came over me."

His hand came up to her neck, lightly massaging the skin underneath her hair. "I think I do. Do you want to tell me about the first attack? We talked about this a little bit, but I don't really know anything about it. I didn't know for sure you'd been raped." He left that thought with her for a little while, continuing to massage her neck, wanting her to know he was here for her.

"It happened at night. I did what I often do. I was so wrapped up in the history books at the library that I didn't pay attention to the time. I'd planned to leave at nine, but it was ten thirty when I finally looked up from my book. It was medieval history, Scottish clan history, and I'd found something about Clan Ramsay. My mother had just married Ryan's father, and I was so curious..."

She took a deep breath, and he gave her the time to gather her thoughts. "I don't have many memories of the incident because I blacked out, fortunately. But I do recall that he dragged me into the bushes..."

"If you don't want to tell me, you don't have to. I don't want you reliving it if it's too painful."

She sat up and stared at him, her hands resting on his chest. "It was dark, he wore a mask, and the only other thing that I remember is that he said he wouldn't allow me to give my virginity to anyone else, that it was *his*."

So her rapist had known her. He wanted to prompt her, to ask her a thousand questions so he could find the bastard and beat him to a pulp, but he was sure the police had covered everything. He would not turn this into an inquisition. He was grateful she'd shared this much with him.

He had something to say to her, something he was struggling to phrase correctly. But he'd get it right if he had to correct himself ten times.

CHAPTER FOURTEEN

LAUREN DIDN'T KNOW HOW NATE would react to her admission. She'd never told any man outside of her family. To her delight, Nate completely surprised her.

His finger reached up to stroke her cheek. "Do not remember that as the day you lost your virginity. Nothing could be further from the truth, in my opinion. Your virginity is *yours* to give away." He brushed a stray hair away from her eye. "That bastard committed a violent act that tore some skin and took your innocence, but he didn't take anything from you. If you haven't done it already, the day will come when you will give yourself to another person for the right reasons, and that man will show you how wrong that bastard was, and how beautiful love can be."

That was the moment Lauren lost her heart to Nate Patterson. And the only thing she could think to say was, "You *are* my Alex."

"What?"

"Nothing. That isn't anyone else's name." He probably thought she was calling him by some ex's name. She hoped she could tell him the truth someday, but she'd opened herself up enough for one night. "It's meant as a compliment. Someone told me once that someday I'd find my Alex, my true..." she stopped. Was she ready to admit she loved him? Maybe not. "Just know I've never dated anyone by that name. It's a compliment."

He laughed, touching his lips to hers briefly. She cupped his face and kissed him, hoping she could silently tell him what she could not yet put it into words. When she teased him with her tongue, he groaned and reciprocated by delving deeper into her mouth, tantalizing her in ways she'd never experienced before. Their kiss went deeper and deeper, driven by the passion of two people who'd been without for a long time. She wanted him in a way that was confusing to her. These were needs she'd thought she didn't have anymore, needs she had repressed for a long, long time.

When he ended the kiss, they were both panting, much to her delight. She'd hoped the desire pumping through her veins was not one-sided.

"Nate, that's the nicest thing anyone has ever said to me," she whispered. "I would like you to be that man."

"Nothing would please me more, but when it happens, I need you to be sure. I don't think this is the right time."

Her hands ran down his chest and then reached for his hands. "You're right. I'm not ready yet. But I trust you, and that has been very difficult for me. Your touch always leaves me wanting more. I hope you'll be patient with me."

"This is completely within your control."

"You promise not to betray my confidence?"

Nate hesitated, but he agreed. "I won't say anything unless your life is at risk. If something like that happens and you're in danger, I'll talk to Ryan, but I won't say anything otherwise. I can't help but wonder why you haven't turned it over yourself."

Lauren couldn't explain what her gut told her. "I can't really answer that. It's just...something tells me I need to hang on to it. Privacy is paramount to support groups. Do you understand what I mean? I'd much rather just figure this out myself."

"I agree with you that the answer is there. Don't you trust Ryan and Jake enough to ask them not to compromise the information? Can't they study it without talking to the victims directly?"

"I don't know. I suppose I can put the question to Ryan. But he could force me to turn it over, and then it'll be out of my hands. And what if his chief insists on taking over? Then Ryan won't have any control over the situation."

Nate leaned over and kissed her forehead. "Promise me to think about it? That's all I ask."

For him, she would. "I'll think about it."

She had this fear that everything would careen into a catastrophe if she lost control of the chart. While she didn't understand why she felt that way, there was no denying she did.

☾

Lauren moved into Stacy's apartment on Thursday. With Nate's help, it only took a couple of hours.

Stacy had taken an instant liking to Nate. "Oh boy," she said after he left, "do you think you can convince him and his buddies to do one of those firefighter calendars?"

It felt wonderful to have some space of her own again, to assert her independence.

Lauren hummed to herself as she headed back to her car after her last class of the day on Friday. While the campus at Summerhill College was always busy, the quadrangle at Cornell was nearly deserted.

She'd almost made her way out of the Science Quad when a woman's voice called out to her from behind.

"Ms. Grant? Lauren Grant?"

She spun around with a lump in her throat and a hand in her bag already reaching for her mace. The first thing she noticed was the fear in the young woman's gaze. "Yes?"

She had long dark hair and looked very young. Lauren waited for her to speak so as not to frighten her away.

"Are you Lauren Grant?"

The girl drew close enough for her to see the tears welling in her eyes, and Lauren's pulse and breathing sped up, though she did her best to slow herself down. She glanced around the quad and noticed several other students wandering about, but they ignored the two women.

Fear needled into her. *Stay calm!* This was a public place, and it was around five o'clock, and the sun shone bright. She was not about to be attacked.

"Yes, I'm Lauren Grant. Are you all right? Has something happened to you?"

The girl's lower lip quivered and she gave a quick nod, her head spinning around to check the area before she brought her attention back to Lauren. "I have a message for you."

"From whom?"

"From one of the frats at Summerhill College. I'm supposed to tell you that I was kidnapped last night because of you. Your brothers need to stop poking around. The investigation has to go away, or they'll attack more women and tell them it's all your fault." Tears slid down her cheeks, and Lauren could see she was about to lose control.

"Let me help you. I can go to the emergency room with you. I can..."

"No!" Her shout carried across the campus. She lowered her voice. "No, please. Nothing has happened yet, so they won't find anything at the hospital. But I'm being watched," she whispered. "I was told I had to give you this message, or they'll assault me tonight. All of them."

"Who? Tell me which frat. Please." Lauren reached for the girl's hand, but she took several steps back. "You need to go to the police. I'll go with you."

"I've never been so scared in my whole life. I'm leaving campus as soon as I do as they instructed. They're animals. I'm sorry, but I...I know they meant what they said, and I can't let them hurt me. Have your brother stop. Please." She lowered her voice and added, "They're also waiting for you. I'm so sorry."

She whirled around and ran down one of the paths toward the parking lot.

"Wait!" Lauren pleaded. "Tell me more, please." If the woman had more information, this could be the break Jake and Ryan needed. But the stranger didn't slow or even stop.

Lauren could feel the wetness of her own tears fill her cheeks. Her first thought was to follow the woman, but she had said *they* were waiting for her. What if they were lying in wait in the parking lot or near the bus stop?

Panic flooded her veins as her gaze darted from one person to the next, then the next, but they all continued on their way as if nothing had happened.

Her feet carried her backward until she hit a bench, and she collapsed onto it, unable to take another step.

The trembling started in her hands and traveled through the rest of her body until even her feet shook. How could she possibly walk home? It was a forty-five minute drive.

Which direction should she go? She was in the middle of the quad, it was still daylight, and she was scared shitless.

Maybe to the parking lot to catch the bus. But that's the direction the girl had gone, and it was undoubtedly where they were waiting.

Maybe back into the class building to find her professor.

No, he'd said he was leaving right away. He'd even canceled office hours.

What time did they lock the buildings up?

What was her address anyway? Where did she live now?

She was losing her mind. She couldn't even recall her new address.

Should she call her mother?

No.

Her heart pounded so powerfully in her chest that she wondered why it didn't just explode inside her and end her misery.

What could she do?

The woman had implied that the frat guys wouldn't attack either of them if Ryan stopped his investigation, but they might still attack her, frighten her, threaten her. She couldn't take that chance.

Nate. Nate would help her if he were here. But he'd said he was picking up a shift today.

Take your phone out and call Nate. Even if he's working, he'll tell you what to do. Or Ryan. Call Ryan.

But Nate had gotten to her first when she'd been attacked last time.

She fumbled with her book bag, locating her phone and pulling it out, and glanced over her shoulder again to make sure no one would bother her.

Afraid to talk, she texted him instead.

Nate, help me.

He answered so quickly, it startled her.

Where are you?

Cornell U in the Science quad

Be right there. Working so I'm coming with the EMT vehicle.

Just come.

She knew he would. Her eyes drifted shut and she tried to recall everything the girl had said. Though she'd been hurt and threatened by members of a frat, she hadn't identified which one. The girl had been frightened half to death.

Just as Lauren was now.

This meant that Ryan was on the right path. She'd been attacked by members of a fraternity, just like he thought.

She jumped up from her seat, recalling the conversation the

guys who'd attacked her had carried on. A new memory had surfaced—a very important one.

"Did you get that?"

The leader had said that to one of the others. That could only mean one thing. One of them had recorded the attack on their phone. They'd taken a picture or a video.

Her phone lit up again, the little jingle calling to her. She breathed a sigh of relief when she saw it was a message from Nate.

Are you all right? We're on our way.

Not hurt. Scared.

Why?

Threatened.

It took her three tries to type that one word into her phone close enough so the auto-correct would pick it up.

The texts kept coming, each one easing the feeling of being alone and afraid.

Ten minutes later, the EMT van pulled up in front of the quad, lights blazing. Or had it been twenty minutes…or five? She really had no idea.

Hurry, Nate.

She managed to stand and look in that direction. There was only one problem.

Her feet wouldn't move.

CHAPTER FIFTEEN

NATE WAS SO WORRIED FOR Lauren, he felt close to vomiting, but he forced himself to place the call officially so he could take the vehicle to campus. He'd be off at seven tonight and it was already well after five.

He yelled to his brother, "Sam, you're driving."

"You'll allow me to drive? What the hell has gotten into you?"

"It's Lauren Grant. I want to keep her texting."

"Shit. Sorry." They grabbed their gear and climbed into the truck. "Where?" Sam asked.

"Science quadrangle at Cornell."

Once they left, sirens blaring, Nate continued the conversation with Lauren.

Sam fired one question after another at him. "What happened? Is she hurt? Do we need to call the ED?"

He began to wonder who was more worried about Lauren, him or Sam. "What the hell is the matter with you? I can't answer everything yet."

"Sorry," he said sheepishly. "I just know how much you like her, and she's been through so much already."

"I know."

"First things first. Is she hurt?" Sam asked.

"I don't think so. She said she was threatened."

He punched another message into his phone, hoping she would stay with him. **Stay where you are. Don't move inside. Stay where others can see you.**

The sick feeling in his gut told him that Lauren was even more important to him than he'd realized.

"You're pretty hot on her, aren't you?" Sam asked, serious for once.

"Yeah." He ran his hand down his face. "I didn't plan on it, it just happened."

"Did she answer you?"

"I didn't ask her anything." He gave Sam a look of exasperation.

His message alert sounded. **I'm in the middle of the quad.**

Alone?

Yes.

Anyone suspicious around you?

Not that I can see. I'm scared because of something someone told me.

Stay where you are. We'll be there soon.

"What did she say?"

"She's alone in the middle of the quad. No one suspicious around, but someone told her something that freaked her out." He stared out the windshield. "What do you think that means?"

"Maybe someone threatened her and took off. Or maybe she received a phone call that was threatening. Could be she recognized someone from the attack. I'll bet that's it."

He didn't want to guess. He just prayed she'd be all right, that they would get there in time.

"You in love with this girl?" Sam asked, his eyes going wide.

He didn't even know how to answer his brother. "I don't know. Damn, the woman has the worst luck of anyone I know."

They pulled into the parking lot closest to the science quad, and he hopped out of the vehicle, hurrying toward the center of the quad. He didn't grab anything, so he yelled to his brother. "Call it in and bring the bag."

He prayed she was okay, that she still hadn't been hurt. He found her in the middle of the quad standing in front of a bench, staring at him with a look that broke his heart. "Lauren?"

"Nate." Her gaze found his. "I can't move."

He stopped in front of her, trained not to touch anyone in case they were strapped to a bomb. "Why not? Tell me what happened."

"A woman gave me a message. She said that I have to speak to Ryan, get him to stop investigating the attacks on me, or they'll hurt me and other women. The woman said they're watching me, and then she ran off, and..."

He held his hands up to her. "Slow down, hon. Slow down."

He could hear his brother coming up behind him. "Is someone watching you now?" He did his best to scan the area without being obvious.

"I don't know. I'm just so frightened that my legs won't move. I was afraid to get on the bus," her tears rushed out. "Afraid to go to the parking lot, or inside, or move at all."

"Where is she?"

"She's gone. She ran to the parking lot, so I was afraid to follow her. I thought they might be waiting there."

"I'm going to touch you, all right?"

She nodded, reaching for him, but he took her wrist instead, catching her racing pulse as soon as he pressed on her wrist. "Sam and I will help you walk over to the vehicle." He motioned for Sam to fall in on her other side. "Do you remember Sam from the party?"

She nodded and grabbed Nate's arm. "I'm so sorry to bother you, Sam."

"Not a bother," he said with a grin. "We were so bored, we were glad for the call."

Nate put his hand at the small of her back and gave her a little push, angling his body behind her in case she collapsed. After a couple of slow steps, he scooped her up into his arms and carried her over to the truck, waiting for Sam to open the back so he could place her on the gurney. She was too upset to follow instructions. He had to keep her from going into shock. Though it was rare, extreme emotional trauma could affect the body so severely that she might faint, hit her head, or experience other serious side effects. He'd seen it happen before.

Once they settled her inside, he said, "I'm taking you to your mother's house."

"No. I need to talk to Ryan. I remembered something important about the attack. Where is he?" She still had her phone clutched in her hand, so she searched for Ryan's number. "Take me to my apartment. Ryan will come to my place."

Nate nodded to his brother. "Head to the place on the lake."

Lauren sat up and shouted, "No. I want to go to my apartment. Don't tell me what to do."

"Where is your apartment, Lauren?" Sam asked.

She didn't answer him.

"Lauren," Nate said calmly, "you need to be with someone. Do you know if Stacy is home? You shouldn't be alone. Let's go to the lake house." Had she no sense of reason? She shouldn't go to a place where she would be alone or where two of them would be alone.

She punched in a message to Ryan, then glared at him. "If I go home, I'll upset my mother, and I'm not going to do that. I don't want to burden her. You don't get to give me orders."

"I'm not trying to give you orders. I'm just trying to help you decide what to do."

"Yes, you are giving me orders. I don't like that," she snapped. "I'm sick of being pushed around."

Not wanting to upset her, he asked, "Let's wait and see where Ryan is."

Her text sounded so she pulled out her phone.

"Do you need a refresher course in trauma training?" Sam asked in an undertone.

Nate countered his brother's comment almost immediately, "She needs to think about what she's doing. She shouldn't be alone." He didn't like the way his own tone and voice had changed.

"And what's wrong with the first part of that sentence?" Sam pressed, his voice calm and determined.

Nate glared at his brother, annoyed because he was exactly right. Trauma victims had no sense. Their bodies were stuck in "fight or flight" mode, which pulled oxygen to the parts of the body that needed it most—the lungs, the muscles, the physical senses. The brain even changed, directing the body to focus on the perceived threat instead of the details. She wasn't capable of thinking reasonably at the moment. He waited to see what Ryan said.

She turned her phone to him so he could see Ryan's response, as if she were afraid to hand it over. "He's with his dad at the lake." She turned around to look at Sam. "You can take me there. I need to see my brother. I'll go along with you this time, Nate."

She turned her head away from Nate, something that broke his heart. He hadn't intended to sound that way, like he was giving her orders. "I'm sorry, Lauren, but I'm worried about you. What exactly did the woman say to you?" He reached for her hand, clasping it with his, hoping she wouldn't pull away. He wanted, no, needed to comfort her.

She took a deep breath and said, "She said she'd been kidnapped by guys in a frat. They blamed it on me, and said they'd continue to attack women, including me, unless Ryan walked away from the investigation."

"What was her name?"

Lauren eyes seemed to go even wider. "I don't know. She never told me... It happened so fast. I called after her, but she didn't answer. She said she was leaving campus today because she was so scared."

"She was as frightened as you are."

"This has to stop. We can't place other women at risk."

"I agree, but Ryan can't back down. It's more important now than ever for us to stop the people who are doing this."

She stared at her hands when her face lit up. "Oh, I remembered something about the attack. I heard the leader of the group ask another one of the guys if he'd gotten it."

Nate's heart leapt to his throat. Could that mean... Would they have been stupid enough to film what they'd done? "Tell me exactly what he said."

She closed her eyes and said, "He asked, 'Did you get that?'"

Somewhere, there was a video of Lauren's attack.

He'd find it. He'd find it, and he'd make them pay.

☾

When they pulled into the driveway, Lauren glanced at Nate. He was upset, she could tell. "Nate, I didn't mean to yell at you. I was upset. I'm sorry."

He opened the doors and hopped out, "It's all right. I was worried about you. But I have to admit, I've been worried about you ever since you moved in with Stacy. Until these guys are caught, I think you'd be better off here."

"Nate, please...don't. I can make my own decisions. I like living with Stacy, and it's nice to be closer to campus. I don't want to let *them* decide how I live my life."

"Can you walk?" He held her wrist, probably checking her pulse so she did her best to stay still for him, something that was nearly impossible.

"Yes."

As soon as she stepped out of the EMT vehicle, the door to the house opened, and Ryan flew out, followed by their parents. "Lauren, are you all right? What happened?"

"I'm fine, but I need to speak with you, Ryan."

Ryan gave her a hug and said, "Of course, I'll help you in any way I can."

He ushered her toward the house and Nate turned to his brother. "It's almost time to clock out. You can go back. I'll have Ryan give me a ride home. Sign out for me? Talk to the chief?"

"Sure." Sam clapped him on the back. He closed the vehicle's back doors and climbed back inside, giving them a quick wave before he departed.

Lauren headed to the back porch with Nate and Ryan, though she was so anxious she couldn't stop her hands from shaking. Her mother ushered her into a seat, and she was extremely grateful when Nate sat next to her and grasped her hand, that small gesture giving her the support she needed so badly. She proceeded to tell Ryan and her parents everything, going into more detail now that the shock had worn off. When she got to the part about her suspicions about the video, Ryan leapt up from his chair.

"Seriously?" he said. "Why do you think that?"

She gave him the exact words the man had used.

Ryan said, "Great job, Lauren. This is exactly the kind of lead we were hoping for. We checked their Facebook pages and all their social media for any pictures or references to your attack—or even to you—and we managed to get access to Randy's phone. We didn't find anything unusual on it."

"Maybe it was a different frat all along," Ryan's father said. "Or someone else recorded it and deleted it."

Nate said, "If they went to the trouble of taking the video, you can be certain it wasn't deleted. Maybe they have a flash drive, or it's stored in someone's cloud account. They wouldn't have recorded it unless they planned on keeping it."

"I agree," Ryan said, still standing. He looked eager to start digging into the new lead. "It's out there somewhere, and Lauren's memory of the incident will allow us to pull a warrant for all the phones of every member and pledge in the two frats we suspect."

"What about the girl who spoke to me?" Lauren asked.

"I'll talk to the chief and see about setting a security watch on all the frats tonight. But without more information, we have no way of knowing who she is or where she's gone. She could have flown halfway across the country by now. But we'll put some pressure on them, let them know we're watching."

"That's exactly what they don't want you to do. It could put her at risk." Even as she said the words, she knew they couldn't back off. They couldn't give these men what they wanted.

"I know, Lauren. But that's not how we handle criminals. We have to keep moving in closer. We'll do our best to be inconspicuous. But we have to be certain she was not taken back to one of the frats."

☾

Nate wanted so badly to tell Ryan that Lauren had put a great deal of effort in recording the details of every attack that had happened in Summerhill in the last couple of years. She had details he was sure the police didn't have. He couldn't betray her, but he could do his best to convince her to turn the chart over to Ryan.

"Lauren," he said carefully, "are you sure you don't have anything else that could help Ryan with his job?"

"No, I can't think of anything else. That's all I remember." She didn't give any indication that she understood the reference.

"Are you sure?" He gave her a pointed look, and this time she blushed, indicating she'd caught on. The look that crossed her face was not pleasant.

"Well, what you've remembered will help us immensely," Ryan said. "That's more than we'd hoped for. If you don't have anything else, I'm going to the department to speak with our chief, and then I'll seek a warrant to go after their phones. I hope we find something." He strode over to Lauren's chair, leaning down to give her a kiss on her forehead. "Why don't you stay here tonight? If I find out anything, I'll let you know."

Lauren glared at him. "I suppose I'll stay here."

Her mother said, "Good. Call Stacy and let her know what happened. She'll understand. I'll fix you something to eat. Ryan, Nate? Would you like a sandwich or something?"

Ryan said, "No. I've got work to do. I'll get something later."

Though Nate had a feeling Lauren was less than pleased with him, and he knew he should probably stay and talk to her, he needed to get a ride from Ryan. "Would you mind giving me a ride home?" he asked. "I sent my brother back to the station to return the vehicle."

"I can take you wherever you'd like to go. Do you want me to drop you off at the fire station?"

Nate glanced at his watch. "No. I'm off the clock. Sam will get the truck. My house will be fine." He leaned over and gave Lauren a quick kiss on her lips, but she didn't respond.

Well, shit.

As Nate followed Ryan out the door, he heard Lorraine say, "If Lauren won't thank you, I will, Nate. Thank you for coming to my daughter's aid again."

Nate could tell the woman was close to tears, so he just turned to her and said, "You're welcome, Mrs. Ramsay. Lauren's had quite a month. I hope we're reaching the end of this." He glanced at Lauren, hoping for some sort of response, but she turned her head. Not knowing what else to do, he left.

He couldn't shake the voices in his head—Sam's and Tristan's and Mandy's—telling him he was overprotective and bossy. Lauren had gotten a taste of that tonight, and it was obvious she didn't like it. Well, what was he to do? He couldn't change the way he was.

Could he?

Once they were on the road, Ryan asked, "Is something wrong between you and Lauren?"

"No, she's just had a traumatic day."

"I hope you're right. I think you two are good together."

"I won't give up. You think you'll be able to do something with this new intel?"

"Yes, I do. You'd be surprised how many criminals feel the need to record their attacks so they can watch them again. I'm guessing the video was saved for one or two people. Could be that someone required a pledge to record the incident. Sometimes students are asked to engage in risky behavior to get accepted into the fraternity. You'd be surprised what kind of things are required of them—not just at Summerhill, but in many schools across the country."

Nate thought about his for a moment, a sad testament to their college culture.

Ryan interrupted his thoughts. "What exactly did you mean when you asked Lauren if she had something else she wanted to tell me?"

"Nothing. I thought she'd said something else..." He was eager to tell Ryan about the chart, but he'd made a promise to Lauren. He couldn't say her life was at risk yet. It wasn't time to break his word to her.

"Are you sure? Because she certainly was upset by your comment. If there's something else that could help us, I'd like to know about it."

Nate sighed. "I made a promise."

Ryan nodded slowly. "That explains it. Think about it. If I didn't have this other information to chase, I'd be coming down on both of you a little harder, but I'm not going to bring her to the station. You need to think really hard about whether keeping that information close to the chest is hindering our investigation." He pulled into Nate's driveway and put his car in park, then turned to level a serious look at Nate. "Withholding information from an active investigation can be a crime, as you know."

Nate said, "I'll talk to her when she's calmer. This wasn't the time to raise the question, Ryan. Trust me on that. Lauren is close to going over the edge, and I'm not going to be the one to push her. My intent is to be there for her so I can catch her if she falls."

Ryan said, "I'll respect that for now."

CHAPTER SIXTEEN

NATE STEPPED INSIDE HIS HOUSE, surprised to see Sam sitting on the couch. Had that much time passed? "Sam." He acknowledged his brother with a nod, then walked over to the fridge to grab a beer.

Sam launched right into it. "There's something wrong with this picture, Nate, and we're going to talk about it."

He spun around to glare at his brother, not in the mood for a lecture after the day he'd had. Hadn't Sam already made his point clear? "What are you talking about?"

"You just got done telling me how much you like this girl, and then you barked orders at her at the worst possible time. The woman was traumatized! Didn't you hear yourself?"

Nate ran his hand through his hair and started to pace, uncomfortable with the accusation. Part of him knew Sam was right, but that didn't mean *he* had been wrong. "She needed to be somewhere she could be watched." The volume of his voice rose as he spoke, his defensiveness kicking in. "Where are those idiot frat boys more likely to attack her? Some small apartment with two women in it or at a huge lake house that could have fifteen people inside at any given moment? Think about it. She's safer at her parents' house right now. She's...she's not thinking clearly."

"Neither are you," Sam said frankly. "The circumstances are irrelevant. You're making the same mistake you made with Mandy."

He started to say something, make some kind of rebuttal, but Sam held up his hands and said, "Look, I'm glad you and Mandy split. You weren't right for each other. I just don't want to see you sabotage another relationship."

"Is that why you countermanded me and asked for the address

of her apartment?"

Sam got up and moved into his brother's face. "I did that because it's my job. I do what people ask me to do. And Nate, it's your job, too. We take people where they want to go unless they're unstable and require emergency treatment, in which case we take them to the nearest hospital."

"We took her to the safest place," Nate insisted, shaking his head.

His brother's face turned red. "Did she give you a hug and a big thank you?" he asked, his voice raising in volume, too. "Because I'm betting she was barely speaking to you by the time you left."

Tristan came in the front door, his eyes wide. "What the hell's gotten into you two? I could hear you from outside."

Sam said, "Nothing new. Just our brother trying to control everyone around him again."

Nate closed his eyes and slumped into the easy chair. Sam was right, he *knew* he'd been a complete ass. What had come over him? He lowered his face into his hands. "You're right. I know you're right. I knew it in the truck, but I couldn't stop myself. She wouldn't even look me in the eye when I left."

Sam sat down on the couch not far from him. "I'd hoped that things might change after you saved that woman in the car accident. That maybe you could finally let go of the past."

He jerked his head to stare at his brother, scowling. "What does that have to do with this?"

"You can't see it, can you?" Sam asked softly.

"See what?"

"That you still feel guilty for Mom's death, when the truth is that there was nothing you or anyone could have done to save her. Her chest was crushed in the accident. Her lungs were collapsing. Even if you'd freed her, you couldn't have stopped the damage that was already done. She was too far gone."

"You don't know that." He bolted back out of his chair and started pacing again, needing an outlet for the nervous energy. He could have saved her. Had he gotten her free, maybe the EMTs could have done something. Maybe her chest hadn't been crushed until the last few minutes. If he'd only gotten to her sooner...

"Yeah, I do," Sam insisted. "I spoke with the EMTs, and I've asked many doctors since then. Even if her lungs hadn't collapsed, her internal injuries would have killed her. The entire front of the vehicle had her pinned in that car. It literally crushed the life out of her, not you."

"Maybe the surgeons could have…"

"Stop, for God's sake. It's time to let it go, Nate. You need to stop torturing yourself."

Tristan, who'd stood watching them, speechless, took a step toward Nate. "He's right. It wasn't your fault. No part of it was your fault. You need to stop trying to fix everything and everyone to make up for it. You're a great EMT and firefighter. You help people every day, and you've done everything you can to keep us together. Look, maybe I don't act like it sometimes, but I appreciate everything you've done."

Nate fell back into the chair. "I know I acted like an ass today. I'm just afraid…I don't want to lose her. She means too much to me already." He stared at his hands. "Maybe I *do* become a little crazy when I think I'm going to lose someone. When that call came in…my mind was wild… I couldn't focus on anything but getting to her."

Tristan sat next to Sam on the couch. "Maybe it's time for you to just enjoy each other," Sam said. "I think Ryan has the investigation under control."

Tristan nodded emphatically. "You're a lot of fun on the volleyball court or boating, but when you're in charge of anything, you kind of suck."

Nate laughed. "Thanks for your blunt honesty, Tristan. I can't disagree with you guys. And as for just enjoying each other? I wish we could." He sighed. "All these mind games they're playing with her…they're taking a toll. It's tough watching her go through this."

"You can't make it all go away any more than you could have fixed Mom," Sam said. "But you can be there to help her get through it."

"I wish I had a nice girlfriend. I'd be kicking you guys out every night for two hours," Tristan said with a grin.

Sam guffawed. "I'm betting it would only take you two minutes, not two hours…"

Tristan glared at him, then burst out laughing. "You're probably right."

"How are your classes?" Nate asked, rubbing his hands together. He had to do better, be kinder, more considerate. He couldn't love the people close to him any more than he already did, but his people skills? Tristan was right. They could use some serious improvement.

"Good. And thanks for making me go the other day. I got matched with a group of beautiful ladies for the accounting project."

They shared a laugh, but Nate's nerves didn't settle. They wouldn't until he fixed things. He grabbed his beer off the coffee table. "Now what do I do? I messed things up today."

"She's probably exhausted," Sam said with a shrug. "I'd let her rest tonight. Text her tomorrow. Try to see her."

He played with the label on his beer, peeling it away in spots. "Maybe the police will have found something by then."

"Just apologize. You were both stressed by the situation. I'm sure she'll understand."

"You're right, but I'm not going to let this lie. I'll call Ryan in the morning. If he hasn't turned anything up by morning, I'll go after the bastards myself."

Nate didn't have to work the next day, so he got up around eight and picked up his phone, trying to decide whether or not it was too early to text Lauren. The house was quiet because Sam had left for work and Tristan was already at the gym. To his surprise, his text alert went off while he held it. A message from Lauren popped up.

Sorry about last night. I appreciate what you did for me.

You're welcome. I have some apologizing of my own to do.

He waited, trying to decide what to say next. He finally chose: **How about breakfast?** It would be easier to talk with her if they were face to face. He didn't believe in the teen-age method of depending on messaging for everything.

Sounds great. Want to go out? I'm not great at making breakfast.

I'm pretty good at it. I can pick you up. He didn't want to apologize in front of the people at Deb's Diner.

Okay. I'm ready any time.

Be there in ten minutes.

He checked the fridge, pleased to see a dozen eggs, sausage links in the freezer and a loaf of rye bread on the counter. Sam had even picked up some fresh blueberries and strawberries.

He hopped in his truck, and to his surprise, Lauren was waiting outside the lake house for him. Had something happened? He jumped out as soon as he saw her. "Is everything all right?"

She gave him a warm smile. "Yes. It's just such a beautiful day, I decided to wait outside for you. There are even a few boats out fishing this morning. I love the sound of boats on the water. It's calming to me."

Unsure of exactly what to do because she'd mostly rejected him last night, he opened the passenger door for her. She stopped in front of him and lifted onto her toes to give him a kiss. "I meant what I said. Sorry about last night."

He kissed her again, needing to convince himself she was no longer upset—and to remind him how sweet she tasted. She smelled of coconut and orange, an unusual combination, but he decided one was from her shampoo and the other from orange juice she must have just had.

Once they were on their way, they made small talk, which suited him fine. He'd rather go into apology mode face to face. It would seem half-hearted if he tried to talk to her while he was driving.

"What's your breakfast specialty?" she asked.

"Scrambled eggs. I hope you like them."

"I love them. It's my favorite breakfast, but I tend to burn them. I'm better at dinner."

"And your specialty?"

"I like to cook big meals. Turkey, mashed potatoes, sweet potato casserole, stuffing…you know. The typical Thanksgiving dinner. Turkey is my favorite meat. Or ham and scalloped potatoes."

"I'd love to try your turkey dinner sometime. Don't invite my brothers, though. Tristan will eat all your mashed potatoes."

Out of the blue, she said, "Ryan called this morning."

"And?"

"They…they found the video on someone's phone. A member of Gamma Delta. He said it's quite clear. They'll be analyzing it today and pulling men in for questioning."

"Lauren, that's wonderful. I hope it makes you feel better."

He glanced at her as he pulled into his driveway. Tears were welling in her eyes. When he shut the engine off, he reached for her hand. "This could end most of your problems. If it turns out this frat is behind the attacks, they'll be shut down immediately."

She nodded, smiling through her tears. "I know. This could all finally be over." She reached for him and fell against him, kissing him with more passion and intensity than she ever had before.

Nate couldn't help but respond to her. Before he knew it, he was nearly lying on top of her, kissing her senseless. She just pulled him closer, only stopping long enough to whisper, "More," the word coming out raspy and full of desire.

Hell, but that one word turned him hard in an instant.

"I want you, Nate. All of you."

He kissed a path down her neck and into the creamy valley between her breasts, peeking out of her V-neck sweater. "Lauren, you are so beautiful. You're driving me mad."

He captured her lips with his again and she moaned, the tiniest of sounds that came from the back of her throat and seemed to travel straight to his cock. Hell, he didn't know if he could stop this time. His hands cupped her breasts, massaging them until he could feel her nipples peak through the soft material of her bra.

Lauren whispered, "Make love to me, Nate."

Her words stunned him, though it was what he wanted, too. More than anything. He pulled away from her. "Lauren, I want that more than I've ever wanted anything, but not here. I...I've fallen in love with you, and that scares the hell out of me, but I want to be a better man for you. If you're sure that you want this, no one is home. We can go inside, and I promise to love you the way you should be loved."

She nodded, "I love you, too. I don't want to wait. Please?"

He wasn't sure what possessed him, but he carried her, princess-style, into the house. He just didn't want to stop touching her. Once they were inside his room, he helped her with her outer clothing, but then stopped to kiss her—a sweet kiss to let her know how much she meant to him.

She turned the kiss passionate, slanting her mouth over his to get more of him. Blood roared through his veins, and he had to struggle to slow down, take this at her pace and not his own.

He kissed a trail from her mouth down her throat until he came to the swell of her breasts, then reached back to the clasp in her bra, freeing her beautiful mounds. Cupping them gently, he watched as her eyes closed in pleasure and then, when he teased her nipples, she tipped her head back in delight. He thought he'd lose it right there just from watching her, from seeing the pleasure she took in his touch, but she completely surprised him. Lifting her gaze to his, she removed her pants and then reached for his shirt, peeling it away from him.

He urged her onto the bed, helping her shed her panties and removing his own pants before climbing in next to her.

"Lauren, if you want to stop, just say so. We'll go only as far as you like."

She didn't hesitate. "I want it all, Nate," she said, running her hands over his bare chest. "I want you now. I love you, Nate. Please don't make me wait."

He didn't argue, instead settling his head between her breasts, taking his time to lave each one until she cried out, her hands gripping his hair. How he wished to bury himself inside her, bring her to a fast peak, and listen to her cries of pleasure, but he vowed to wait. He noticed a couple of bruises still visible, so he kissed them as delicately as he could.

What would be the best way?

He finally stopped and said, "Touch me. I want you to know me, not be afraid of me."

She slid her hands down his abdomen to his arousal, gripping him and wrapping her hand around him as he groaned, closing his eyes. "I don't want you to fear me."

"I don't. I trust you completely, Nate. The only thing I worry about is your weight on me. If I feel like you're overpowering me, I'm afraid I'll react because it's the memory I hated most. Just tell me what to do. I'm confused..." she panted, apparently lost in her own need.

Pleased to hear her passion, he rolled onto his back and said, "I want you to be completely in control of the situation. Why don't you be on top, then you can stop whenever you want. We'll go at your pace." He reached for the drawer of his nightstand and drew out a condom. After he rolled it on, he reached for the juncture between her thighs, pleased to feel how much she wanted him. "Straddle me."

She got up on her knees and did as he asked, and he guided

her to the best position, settling her above his erection. "Feel me, rub yourself against me lightly. Tease yourself however you want. I want you to feel good, Lauren." He reached for her breasts, caressing her and tweaking her nipples as she writhed against him. At first she was hesitant, but she soon picked up her own rhythm.

She caught his gaze and rasped out, "This feels so right, Nate."

He reached for her hips and said, "Guide me inside you." Once she completely sheathed him, he closed his eyes and groaned at how tight she was, how slick she was for him. "Set your pace," he managed to say, holding her hands as she brought him in even further until he thought he'd explode.

CHAPTER SEVENTEEN

LAUREN GASPED WHEN SHE WAS fully seated on him, her eyes widening with surprise at the pleasure of feeling him so deep inside her. She'd never imagined it could be like this. "Oh my, Nate. You feel wonderful inside me."

"Finish it, love."

She could tell he was doing his best to control his urges, so she began a pulsating rhythm over him, driving him in as deep as she could, over and over until she wanted to scream. He reached for her clit, and she cried out as his touch sent her over the edge. So many sensations reeled through her that she called out his name, clutching him as she climaxed, her needs rolling in waves as her body convulsed on him.

When she was able, she looked at him as his entire body turned rigid and he finished with a roar inside her. She was barely able to collapse onto him as he brought her down to his side, cradling her, kissing her forehead as they both sought to calm the storm that had raged between them.

Lauren curled on her side and tucked her head onto Nate's shoulder. She'd finally experienced how the physical part of love was supposed to be between two people. All she could do was sigh with pleasure.

"No regrets?" he asked, leaning down to kiss her forehead.

She tipped her head back, staring at this man who had just shown her how much he cherished her. "None. Did I please you?"

"You couldn't tell? Shall I say immensely? Yes, this was wonderful. And for you? Did you enjoy it?"

"Yes. It was much more than I ever expected."

He rubbed his thumb across her cheek, just the way she liked.

"I want to tell you something if you have a few minutes to listen."

"I do. I would love to know more about you. Everything."

"I…I should have told you before, but I'm not good with words. I want to try to explain why I was such an ass before. I shouldn't have tried to tell you what to do." He took a deep breath and sighed.

She vowed to give him all the time he needed, not to judge him, and to be a good listener.

"My mom died in a car accident, and I was in the car with her. My leg was injured in baseball practice, so I was in the back seat. It started pouring out and she went into a skid near the bridge on West Avenue. We hit the bridge a couple of times before the car went across the street and flipped on its side, pinning her inside the vehicle.

"I went crazy. I heard someone outside call 911, so I got out of my seat and tried to save her, but I couldn't. She told me I had to get out because my father couldn't handle losing both of us. She told me to take care of my brothers, as if she knew she was going to die."

"Oh, Nate." She gripped his hand and kissed his cheek.

"I tried so hard to free her, but her chest was pinned by the steering wheel. When the EMTs arrived, one of them lifted me out of the way. I could see her breathing was different, and I'm sure I yelled at them to get her out, but they couldn't. I watched her take her last breath, and I couldn't do a damn thing about it."

"I'm so sorry. What an awful experience for you. That's why you're so protective of your brothers, isn't it?"

"Yeah. I had to make sure they both graduated."

"How long ago was it?"

"I was eighteen, seven years ago."

"I'm twenty-four, a year behind you. Why don't I remember you in high school?"

"Because I was a scrawny wimp."

She giggled. "Well, I was a history geek."

He kissed her again and said, "My sweet geek."

She snuggled against him, running her fingers down his chest.

He sighed again, "Sam thinks that's why I tried to control you, that I couldn't help my mother so I'm always trying to save other people. Protect them." He ran his fingers through her hair.

"He could be right. That's something that will affect you the rest of your life. I'm sure you've talked to enough medical personnel to know you couldn't have done anything more than you did."

"I have spoken with several. They all said internal injuries are often deadly."

She rested her head on the pillow so she could gaze straight into his eyes. "I think your mother would want you to forgive yourself."

"That's what my counselor says. I can't argue with that. She was a great mom, and I know she would have loved you. She always wanted a daughter." He paused. "Do me a favor and talk to me if you ever feel like I'm being too controlling or overprotective? I'm going to try my best to fight it…to get beyond it, but I know it won't go away overnight."

"Deal."

"I want this to work—I want *us* to work. I can't stand the thought of losing you."

"I feel the same way. And know that I love you even more for being so open with me."

His stomach made a loud sound. He gave her a sheepish grin. "Are you still interested in breakfast?"

"I'm starving, so the answer is yes. Can I help you?"

He climbed out of bed and said, "I'll be in and out of the bathroom in five minutes, if you don't mind. Then it's all yours, and I'll meet you in the kitchen. If you make it in time, you can help me with the toast. Does that work for you?"

She nodded. He kissed her, then climbed out of bed and padded down the hall in the nude. Men just had no shame. She huddled under the sheets, letting herself bask in the feeling of being happy and in love. She breathed in his scent still on the pillow. Though she couldn't quite describe it, she now recognized that scent as Nate.

Could this happiness really be hers?

True to his word, he was out of the shower and out of the bathroom in five minutes. He stuck his head into the room and tossed her a towel, his hair curling on his head. She wondered if it would be all curls if he wore it long. "I can't promise we have the nicest towels, but they're clean. That's Sam's job, and he does a pretty good job at keeping the bathroom clean. I can't promise the same with the kitchen. That's my job."

She took the towel and wrapped it around her, taking her clothes with her and heading to the bathroom. While she'd already showered, she appreciated the towel. She wanted to freshen up a bit before breakfast. Several minutes later, she entered the kitchen to the smell of sausage in the frypan.

"May I help? I'll take care of the toast and set the table."

"I'd like nothing better than for us to work together," he said with a grin.

She jumped right in, enjoying the fun of preparing a meal with him. They puttered around each other, comfortable despite the silence, until they sat down to eat. Their plates were heaping with eggs, sausage, toast, and berries.

"Nate, this looks wonderful. I love blueberries."

"Thank Sam for that. He keeps us healthy. Tristan is all about junk food, and I try to be better than when I was his age."

She took a forkful of eggs and almost moaned in pleasure. "The eggs are delicious." It tasted like he'd used just a touch of cheese.

"So do you accept my apology for last night?"

"Of course. We were both upset. I get it. As I said before, I owe you an apology, too."

Her phone rang, which made her jump. One glance at the screen and she said to Nate, "It's Ryan. I'm going to answer it."

He nodded and started to clear the table of the breakfast plates, setting them by the sink.

"Hi, Ryan." She gritted her teeth, hoping he had more good news for her.

"Lauren, can you come down to the station? We need you to take a look at something."

"Sure, I'll be there in fifteen minutes. Is that okay?"

"Do you need me to pick you up?"

"No, I'm having breakfast with Nate. He can bring me, I think." She turned to catch his gaze and he nodded in agreement. "Yes, he'll bring me. Ryan, this isn't a line-up, is it? You know I didn't get a good look at any of the guys. I'd never be able to pick them out."

"No, this is a formality. I'll fill you in when you get here, but we've been able to identify several of the men, and the college is assisting us."

She hung up and repeated everything to Nate.

He left what he was doing and wrapped his arms around her, holding her tight. "This is it. This could be over for you. Maybe we'll finally be able to leave it all behind."

How she hoped he was right.

☾

By the time they walked into the police station, Lauren was trembling. Somehow the visit to the station made it feel so much more real. Nate held her hand—a lifeline—and she had to remind herself to stop squeezing him so tight.

Ryan greeted her as soon as they stepped inside. The Summerhill Police Department was not huge, but their jurisdiction did sometimes involve Summerhill College, though the college had their own security. "Follow me." As they moved down the hallway, Ryan continued, "We've spent quite a bit of time working with security at the college, and they've been more than helpful. We all want to end this before another attack happens. I made them aware of your incident at Cornell yesterday, but we didn't uncover anything unusual last night. I hope the victim went straight home, wherever that is for her."

Ryan was all business when he was in his uniform, but she trusted him completely, so she followed him without question or comment. He brought them into a room that had no furniture other than a table surrounded by chairs and a small desk piled with equipment in the back. A projection screen had been rolled down across from the table.

Ryan introduced her to his police chief. No one introduced the man at the desk, though he nodded to her in a friendly manner.

The chief then took over.

"Lauren, we've uncovered a video that shows a woman being attacked by a group of men. Ryan had reported this to us when it happened, but we need you to tell us that the woman in this video is indeed you, that this was not something in which you were willingly involved. I apologize if that sounds crass, but it has been suggested that this was being filmed for a college production. Do you understand what we're asking you?"

"Yes." She gripped Nate's hand and Ryan nodded to her, his way of showing support.

"Please have a seat. I apologize for any discomfort it may cause you, but we'll have to play the video in its entirety. Please let me know when you're ready." She took the seat at the center of the table, and Nate sat directly beside her, sliding his chair even closer to hers and holding on to her hand.

The chief instructed Ryan to stand off to the side, and as soon as he moved, Lauren nodded. "I'm ready."

Someone dimmed the lights, and the video started on the screen in front of her. It picked up as soon as she was pushed into the trees. The picture was crisp considering the weather conditions and the rain. It had been shot at an angle that did not show the cars in the lot or any of the men's faces. They'd obviously all established beforehand where the person taking the video would stand, so they all turned their backs to the camera.

She took a deep breath and vowed to remain calm.

But she couldn't. The visual brought it all back to her. Unable to stop herself, she jumped out of her chair. Nate followed her, so she leaned over to clutch his arms. She saw hands on her breasts, hands on her pants—tugging and pulling and touching—all while they laughed. Punches and kicks.

She also noticed something else that made her cry.

How hard she had fought.

In the video, she kicked and spat and screamed and squirmed, grabbing her mace can and spraying it, hitting three men with it, causing them to swear and swing at her.

Every time a fist hit her, she reacted with a yell, and before it ended, she was sobbing and sobbing, gripping Nate, who had his arms around her shoulder. Ryan had edged close enough to keep her from falling, but his jaw was clenched tight, and she could tell he was holding himself back. With difficulty.

"Bastards. Those bastards..." Her last words came out in a gut-wrenching sob. The video came to an abrupt halt, but not before she saw something that brought back another memory.

When the lights came back up, Nate helped her back into the chair beside him, while Ryan stayed behind her and lowered his hands to her shoulders—a silent show of support.

The chief said, "Officer Ramsay, I need you to step away from her. Please stand in the back."

Ryan did as he was instructed, but Nate didn't loosen his grip on her hand.

"I apologize for how upsetting that was for you, but are you able to answer a few questions for me, Lauren?" the chief asked.

"Yes," she said, her hand swiping at the tears that refused to stop.

"Is the person being attacked in this video you?"

"Yes."

"Can you tell me where and when this happened?"

She gave him the location, the date, and the time.

"Did you commit to this activity of your own free will?"

"No, I did not. I was walking to my car after studying at Summerhill College library, and one of them came at me from behind, shoving me into the others, forcing me into the trees. I was trying to get into my car."

The chief held his hand up to indicate that was all he needed to hear.

"Did you know any of these men or can you name any of them?"

"No, I cannot."

The chief said, "Is there anything at all that you can tell us that could help us identify any of these men?"

Her heart started to sink, but something in the video had sparked a memory, and if she was right…

Lauren stood up again. "Yes, there is, Chief."

His expression assured her that she had his attention.

"Proceed," he said, raising his eyebrows.

"Can you stop the video when I tell you?"

The chief glanced at the man running the equipment in the back. "Sure can. Just hold your hand up when you want me to stop it."

"Do you need the lights off, Lauren?" the chief asked.

"Yes." Once they complied and her eyes had adjusted, she said, "Go ahead."

She glanced at Nate, who squeezed her hand and leaned over to kiss her cheek. Soaking in additional strength from his nearness, she faced the screen just as the video started to play. She forced herself not to react to the cruelty or the harsh memories it evoked. Midway through, she held her hand up.

The video stopped. There were no faces in the video, but this was the scene when the leader had taken his glove off to slap her.

"What is it, Lauren?" the chief asked.

"There," her finger pointed to the center of the video. "He took his glove off. There's a tattoo on the inside of his left wrist. It's a snake, and I remember the initial D. If you enlarge it, you'll see what I'm talking about. I didn't remember until I saw him remove his glove."

The chief nodded to the man in the back.

They all watched as the visual in front of them grew and grew.

And suddenly there it was—a snake with the initials D. A. M.

Nate whispered, "Dominic A. Miller."

CHAPTER EIGHTEEN

THE FOLLOWING WEEK, LAUREN WAS leaving her favorite class when someone approached her from behind, startling her. "Lauren!"

It was Trevor, Dom's friend. The sight of him sent a shiver down her back. "I just want to say how sorry I am that you were hurt by people I had considered friends." Randy Brooks and another guy—Glenn something—were with him. She remembered him vaguely, though he was a few years younger than her. He'd always given her a creepy vibe. "Dom and the other guys who attacked you got arrested last night, exactly as they should have been."

"Yeah. Because of you, our fraternity is being shut down."

"Shut up, Randy." Trevor shut the other man down quickly, but that didn't stop Randy from glaring at her.

"You got what you wanted," Glenn said, staring at her in a way that instantly made her uncomfortable.

Lauren turned away. "I'm not going to listen to this," she said over her shoulder.

"No, wait," Trevor shouted. He took a few steps toward her so she stopped to hear him out. The other two stayed behind. "I meant what I said. I'm older than the others. They're still in their last year of school. The purpose of the brotherhood was never to hurt people. Dom and the others deserved what they got. I guess I should grow up and move on. I graduated two years ago. Time for me to act like it."

"Thank you, Trevor. I have to go." She spun on her heel and left. Trevor had always seemed nicer than the others, but she didn't plan on having a conversation with him.

Truthfully, she was kind of shocked Randy wasn't part of the group that had attacked her outside the library. According to Ryan, Dominic had confessed to planning her attack, "just for fun," though he'd mentioned her work with the support group. They'd made all the arrests after one of the youngest pledges had confessed everything. His only part had been filming the video, and once his very rich parents had learned of his involvement, his lawyer had traded the names for his freedom as long as he left the area, promising never to return.

He'd been more than happy to squeal and then run.

No one had admitted to starting the fire yet, but everyone was confident the case would break soon.

She couldn't stop thinking about the attack as she drove home, and when she arrived at her apartment, she was quick to lock the door behind her. Stacy was seated at the kitchen table studying. "Hey, you look like you've seen a ghost again. Everything okay?"

She fell into one of the other chairs and said, "Not really. Some of the other frat members stopped me in the quad to apologize to me, and…" Something dawned on her. Why hadn't she thought of it before?

"What is it?"

"It was Trevor, Randy, and Glenn. None of them attend class at Cornell, and Trevor graduated from Summerhill a while ago. I wonder why they were on campus?"

"I wouldn't worry about it. They'd be foolish to threaten you now. I'm sure you already have all the news from your stepbrother, but you have to see the article I found on Facebook." She rotated her laptop so Lauren could read it. "It talks about the arrests they made yesterday. It's a relief they got all seven of them."

Lauren skimmed the post from the local news. The guys who'd hurt her were all in jail. "Gamma Delta's gone. They're actually gone."

Stacy rubbed Lauren's arm. "I've already heard plenty of stories about how awful they were, especially to women. I'm proud of you. You stuck with this and put an end to a severe blight on Summerhill's campus. Congratulations. Is Nate home? You should call him."

"No, he's working today."

Stacy grinned. "You two are so stinking cute together. If he has any single firefighter friends, I wouldn't be opposed to meeting them," she said with a wink.

Lauren couldn't help but laugh. "He's pretty wonderful. I'll let him know. He *does* have a brother who works with him, by the way." A jaw-cracking yawn surprised her. "Ugh. I guess I'm more tired than I thought."

"No wonder, given what you've been up to. Shutting down dangerous frats. Kissing a hot fireman." This time Stacy's smile was more contained. "Why don't you go lie down for a bit?"

"Maybe you're right. I didn't sleep well last night. I think I'll try to get a nap in before I start my paper."

She gave Stacy a hug and moved into her room.

The arrests had lifted a weight off her shoulders. They'd most likely already arrested the person who'd burned down her rental house, though hopefully enough evidence would emerge for them to level charges for that incident, too. With that group out of the way, plus the timely action taken by the college, maybe the cases of abuse would decrease on campus. With any luck, each meeting of her support group would be smaller and smaller.

She pulled out the manila envelope she'd hidden under her mattress, removing it from its case and unfolding the chart so she could look at it one more time. Ultimately, there'd been no need to give it to Ryan. They'd solved it without her.

She glanced over the details, noting how many of the attacks had been made around Gamma Delta. Some of the women had even mentioned Gamma Delta by name.

But she hated to admit that it didn't fit for all of them...some of the women had been attacked a long way away from Gamma Delta, under much different circumstances.

She sighed, realizing that there was no way all the crimes on her chart could have been committed by the same group. Of course, she'd known that on some level, but she hated the thought that there were some men still walking free.

She rested her head on her arm as she lay to the side of the chart, remembering the dream she'd had a while ago about the blonde woman who'd told her that Nate was her Alex. She'd been right about that. Nate was the man for her. She'd love to have the opportunity to thank the blonde woman for her help.

Her eyes drifted close as she fell asleep, exhausted.

She awakened to the lovely woman again. Just like before, they stood in the beautiful, ancient hall. Her eyes took in the large room filled with trestle tables. A huge hearth sat at the end, cushioned chairs arranged in a semi-circle around the warm fire. It put her in mind of the illustrations she'd seen in the books she'd studied—the famed great halls of medieval Scottish castles. Could it be…?

"Thank you for opening your heart to me again," the woman said in a soft voice.

"I'm not sure how I did that," Lauren asked in wonder.

"You said you wished to have the opportunity to thank me. Well, here I am."

Lauren wasn't afraid of her this time. "Are you truly related to me?"

"Aye. A many times over great grandmother."

Everything about the woman was beautiful—her hair, her blue eyes, and her deep blue velvet gown, but mostly her aura of warmth and kindness. Lauren wanted to stay near her and never go back to the waking world.

"Oh, but you must return. We are not nearly ready for you yet. You have much to do first. You have a path to follow, my dear. It's our job to guide you stay on that path to serve the greatest good—to bring your talents to the world."

That was much deeper than Lauren could handle at the moment. She shook her head a little to express her lack of understanding.

"Oh, someday you'll understand. Now, what is it you wished to say to me?"

"Thank you for giving me advice about Nate," Lauren said with a smile. "He's wonderful."

"He is much like my Alex—strong, confident, wise, gentle, and a compassionate warrior. You will be verra happy together."

"Alexander Grant? Was he the one who fought in the Battle of Largs?"

The woman replied, "Aye, you've found him in your books. Alex saved me from a most horrific existence. He is the love of my life, just as Nate will be the love of yours. They both possess the three most important characteristics necessary for love."

"I know honorable is one, but what are the other two?" Lauren didn't know if the woman would answer her, but she thought she'd try. She had her own beliefs but wished to hear more about the medieval view of marriage.

"I'm sure you could tell me one. Why don't you try?"

Lauren sighed, a smile crossing her face as she thought of all the reasons she loved Nate. She knew there was one quality that was of paramount importance to her. She never could have entered into the relationship without it. "Trust. I had to trust Nate completely, or I never could have entered into a relationship with him."

"Aye, you know two of them: honorable and trustworthy. The third has two facets to it. Most people would just say a man simply needs to be loving, but you and I know there is another part to it. Do you understand what I'm saying?"

Lauren thought for a moment, reflecting again on all of the things she loved about Nate. He was hard-working and he made her laugh. He was warm and giving and nurturing, and she knew without a doubt that he would be a wonderful father someday. She said as much to the woman in the blue dress.

"All wonderful characteristics and true, but I needed someone gentle first and foremost. My Alex is probably the strongest man I know, and he was the greatest swordsman of our time, yet he could be as gentle as the soft caress of a feather. He would carry our babes around on his chest, lull them to sleep with just a touch of his thumb to a cheek."

Lauren immediately thought of Nate's gentle caresses, and how he'd held her in the hospital after her attack outside the library. She'd wondered how such a callused hand could be so tender.

"You understand my meaning—gentle and loving is the third quality. They go together for me. They are the finest of qualities, and Nate possesses them all."

While Lauren wished to know more about Alex, she had one more important question she needed to ask, so she pressed onward. "Before you gave me two pieces of advice, but I can't recall the first one."

"I know, 'tis why I was allowed to return to you. You must give the chart to Ryan."

"But why? They've arrested the men who attacked me. Why shouldn't I keep it?"

"The police can use it to solve other crimes. You have no more use of it, do you?" She approached Lauren, not stopping until she was close enough to touch her. Then she reached over and caressed Lauren's cheek. "Let it go. Give it to Ryan. 'Tis best for both of you."

She cupped Lauren's face and kissed her forehead. "Wonderful times are coming soon. Trust me."

☾

Lauren's eyes flew open and she sat up in her bed. She'd had that dream again, only now she remembered the thing she'd forgotten.

The chart.

She folded it back up and returned it to the envelope, sealing it and placing Ryan's full name on the front. Then she went to her desk and retrieved the flash drive that contained the same information.

Lauren carried both out to the table, taking a seat across from Stacy. "If you have a moment, I'd like to share something with you."

Stacy stopped typing on her laptop and said, "Sure. You have my complete attention."

"I know this sounds really strange, but..." she sighed. Part of her wanted to shut down, but she remembered what the blonde woman said. This was important. "I made a chart of all the abused women who came to my support group. I kept track of every attack, every victim, everything they told me about their attackers. I compiled it into one large document, and I also made a copy of it on this flash drive." She said lifting it up to show her.

"Oh, Lauren," she said, rising from her chair to move to the other side to enfold her in a warm embrace. "I can only imagine how hard it was for you do that. What a good idea, though. Did it help the police with this case?"

She blushed and said, "I never gave it to them, but I'm going to do that now."

"What? Why? Oh my..." Stacy said, "I think you're making the right move. You need to share this document. Heck, if it's anywhere near as meticulous as your coursework, it'll help them catch another seven offenders." She moved back to her chair, shaking her head over the situation.

"I suppose." She stared off into space, wondering how she'd explain it to Ryan. Now that she was actually doing something about it, her insistence on holding off seemed ridiculous.

"Not that it matters, but can I ask what changed your mind? You look very confused. How can I help? Oh, sorry. Too many questions. My mind's in a million places."

"It's all right." She paused, thinking it over. Stacy had a very open mind—in the past, the two had had conversations about past lives and other "airy, fairy" stuff, to quote one of her brothers. Something told her that her friend would understand if she shared the truth. "Well," she continued, "I had a dream. Actually, two dreams. A woman who looked like an angel came to me. She said she was my many times removed great grandmother, and she told me two things. The first is that Nate and I were meant to be together."

"Well, I think she's right about that," Stacy said with a grin as she sat down again. "And the second?"

"She said I have to give this chart to Ryan… Do you think I'm crazy?"

"Never." Stacy got up from her chair and walked over to lift Lauren out of hers.

Lauren chuckled. "You don't have to keep getting up for me."

"Yes, I do. I cannot believe all you've been through, and this is even more of a testament to your strength. A lesser person would have fallen apart from all the pressure." Wrapping her arms around her and hugging her tightly, she said, "You're not crazy. Who am I to say whether or not you have a guardian angel who came to you in your dreams? I will tell you this. I *do* believe we have guardian angels who try to guide us in certain directions. Most of us don't listen though. I'm glad you're paying attention. Not to change the subject, but are you still seeing that counselor?"

"Yes. I have an appointment this week." She stepped away from her friend, comforted by Stacy's acceptance.

"You should share all of this with her. You'll feel better about it. In fact, *I* feel better knowing you have an angel following you. I hope it's true. Oh…and that I have one too."

Lauren chuckled. "My angel didn't know what she signed up for, did she?"

"To root for a lovely, kind, and wonderful human being?" Stacy asked, giving her a playful shove. "Give the chart to Ryan. Do you want me to go with you?"

"No, I'll be right back. Oh. Will you keep this flash drive for me? Just in case…you know."

"Sure. I'll put it in a safe place in my desk. If you ever want it back, let me know."

Lauren gathered her things and headed out the door. She'd had to park a distance away from her apartment because there'd been no closer spots. After she scanned the area for safety concerns, she pulled her phone out to text Nate. She knew he'd be pleased with her decision.

Taking my chart to Ryan. Hope you're having a good day.

Yep. Glad you made that decision. :) **Can't wait to see you tonight.**

She smiled at his response and put her phone back into her purse, heading toward her car. It felt so good not to be a nervous wreck every time she stepped outside.

The thought was still lingering in her mind as she opened her car door, though it faded from her mind the moment someone grabbed her from behind. Another car had pulled up next to her. She tried to scream, but a cloth came up to cover her mouth and her nose, something with a strange odor.

Then her world turned dark.

CHAPTER NINETEEN

NATE WAITED ABOUT A HALF an hour before he texted Lauren again. He couldn't help but worry about her. Yes, she was incredibly strong, but she'd been through more ordeals than most people. Sam enjoyed reminding him—annoyingly often—that it was because he was in love.

He couldn't argue.

He was trying his best not to be controlling, but that didn't mean he couldn't text her to see how she'd made out.

Everything go okay with Ryan?

Nothing. He gave her a few more moments in case she was busy talking with her stepbrother.

Lauren, is everything all right?

No answer.

He rubbed the back of his neck, thankful they weren't on a call at the moment. The day had been uneventful. No matter. He had Ryan's personal cell phone number.

Ryan, is Lauren with you?

No. Why?

Have you seen her? She was on her way from her apartment to see you about thirty minutes ago.

No, I haven't seen her.

She's not answering my texts.

Shit. I'm taking the patrol car to her apartment. Call her.

Nate dialed her number, but that sick feeling in his gut told him she wouldn't answer. Fortunately, he had Stacy's number, so he dialed her next.

She picked up right away.

"Stacy, it's Nate. do you know where Lauren is?"

"Yeah, she went to see Ryan."

"I tried to text her, and she's not answering. Ryan says she never made it there. Was she driving or taking the bus?"

"She said she was driving," Stacy asked, her voice shaking a little. "She said her car was parked down the street. I'll check if I can see it."

"I'll hold." His insides felt like they'd explode. Where the hell could she be? It wasn't like Lauren to be distracted, especially from something so serious. It wasn't like she'd leave that chart in the car to go shopping. This was bad. Someone had gone after her. His mind darted back and forth to different possibilities. Had she been beaten and abandoned? Kidnapped? Worse?

He heard sounds the occasional car engine in the background, which told him Stacy was outside.

"Oh, no," Stacy muttered, the words full of horror.

"What is it?" His stomach revolted, but he managed to keep it together.

"Her car is still here. Her purse is inside the car, but it's unlocked and the chart is on the seat. The car keys are on the ground. She... she never would have left it like that."

"Thanks, Stacy. Ryan is on his way in the police car. Don't touch anything, just wait for him to get there." As soon as he hung up, he ran into the chief's office. "I have to go. Lauren is missing. She was supposed to drive to see her brother, but her roommate found her keys on the ground next to the car, and her purse was inside."

The chief shook his head. "With her history, that's not good. We're slow. Take the van, run the siren."

"Thanks, Chief." He didn't wait to be told twice. As he chased into the garage, he heard a voice behind him. "Keep me posted." He flew out the door and hopped into the vehicle, opening the station doors so he could fly out.

An eternity later, or so it seemed, he pulled onto Lauren and Stacy's street. He could see Ryan talking with Stacy. His brother, Jake, stood beside the police cruiser. Nate jumped out of the van almost before he put it in park. "Do we have any leads?"

Jake shook his head, his hands on his hip. "It's not good. All indications are she's been kidnapped. We've got a team coming out to check for fingerprints, but her keys were probably in her hand when they dropped to the ground, so they won't show anything.

Doesn't help that they landed in a puddle. We're still combing the area for any clues, but nothing's come up so far."

The two moved over to where Ryan and Stacy stood on the sidewalk. He and Jake had arrived just in time for the end of the conversation, apparently.

Stacy handed a flash drive to Ryan. "She was going to the station to give you the original chart in that envelope in the car. This is a copy of it. It's something she's been working on for a very long time. She asked me to keep the flash drive in case..." Her breath hitched. "In case anything happened. Oh my God, how could this be happening to her again?"

"What's on the drive, Stacy?" Ryan asked, while Jake headed to the car to retrieve the envelope.

Tears flooded down her cheeks as she struggled for words. Nate knew exactly how she felt—*helpless*. They all did.

"I know what it is," Nate answered. "I've seen the chart. She kept detailed records of all the victims and their attacks, anyone who'd ever come to her support group. She was afraid revealing the information would compromise the integrity of her group, so she kept it secret. Trust me that there are many entries on this. Around fifty." Damn, why the hell hadn't he made her turn that over to Ryan when he'd first learned about it? He knew why. He hadn't wanted to lose her, and the news of the video had seemed far more pressing.

"She had records and she didn't give them to me before?" Ryan asked. Both he and Jake were staring at Nate in bafflement.

"That's what I almost told you about when you gave me a ride home, but she made me promise not to tell you."

"And you listened to her?" Jake asked, incredulous, putting gloves on to pull the envelope out of the car.

"The hard copy is in that envelope you're holding." Nate pointed to the manila. "Ryan, I told you I wanted her to come to this decision on her own...and she finally had. That's why she was coming to see you. Shit!" He ran his hand down his face. "Big mistake, I know."

Ryan took the envelope from Jake, both of them handling it with gloves on. Somehow he managed to get it out without manhandling the envelope. Another vehicle had arrived on scene without Nate even processing it—and one of the guys took the envelope from Jake and placed it inside a plastic evidence bag.

Ryan unfolded the chart part way, enough to see the contents of the document. "Holy shit."

Jake peeked over Ryan's shoulder. "Everything…everything is there. More than we have."

"Why would it be more than what the police department has?" Nate asked. Had he known that, he might have been more insistent. He'd expected it to be almost the same.

"Because some of the victims refused to speak to the police. That's why Lauren started the support group, to help the women who were too afraid to talk to us. This is magnificent," Ryan said, scanning it again. "Unfortunately, it will take us a while to go over it."

"We don't have a while," Nate insisted hotly. "Tell me who you arrested, because the report I saw didn't list all the names, only Dominic Miller. What about the others we saw? Randy, Trevor?"

"She mentioned a Glenn, too," Stacy added. "A few of those guys stopped her before she came home today."

"Which ones?" Jake pressed. "This could be important. Think carefully, Stacy."

Stacy closed her eyes for a moment, then opened them back up. "Glenn was one, but she also mentioned a Trevor and a Randy. She said they all attended Summerhill College, but she ran into them on the Cornell campus."

"That's revealing. They have no business at Cornell. Trevor Hutton doesn't live with the frat," Ryan said. "He graduated a couple of years ago. He lives on the lake with his parents, though they're only there half the year. They're snowbirds, so they'll be heading south soon. He wasn't part of that group. Besides Dom, the kids we arrested were all pledges. They've all been expelled."

"In other words," Nate said, "the frat is pissed. Several of their friends are expelled and the fraternity was shut down."

"Exactly," Jake said. "And expect to see more frats closed. We're still going after the other one we suspected of malicious misbehavior. I'm sure this document will help incriminate them, but only if the victims are willing to testify."

"That unfortunately gives us a lot of suspects," Ryan said.

"Randy Brooks?"

"He had an alibi for the night of the library attack," Jake said.

Ryan said, "We're returning to the department. Nate, join us. We'll put out an APB for Lauren and come up with a plan in the squad room."

Nate nodded and climbed back in his vehicle, but he didn't like it.

He needed to search for Lauren now. They couldn't afford to take their time.

It could mean life or death for her.

☾

The first thing Lauren sensed when she came to was the foul taste of the coarse gag in her mouth. A horrible, discomfiting grogginess wrapped around her senses, making everything seem cloudy and strange. She opened her eyes and scanned the area around her, confused. She was on a small bed and the room had a low ceiling with small windows. As soon as she moved her hands to push herself up, she discovered the bindings tying her hands together and her feet together. The memory of going to her car with the chart came back to her. The person who'd grabbed at her from behind...

A voice broke through her confusion. "I'm glad you're awake, sweetheart."

The man leaned over and kissed her forehead, but she pulled away.

"It's all right. I know you're frightened. Understand that I'll never hurt you. I just needed to bind you and gag you to get you away from there. Too many of your brothers and stepbrothers are military and policemen."

He sat down on a stool next to her cot, and the proximity to her attacker made her want to vomit. She recognized him, and if she could ask him just one question, it would be: *Why?*

"I know. I've surprised you, haven't I? It's really quite simple. I love you, just as I've always loved you." He stood up and walked away, leaning against the wall and then turning to face her with his arms crossed. "I've loved you ever since high school. But you didn't even know I existed. And when I finally got the nerve up to invite you to the prom, you turned me down." He said it with the calmest composure she'd ever seen before. Then he picked up a long piece of wood and slammed it down on the counter behind him. "You. Turned. Me. Down." The last came out in such a growl that she curled into as much of ball as her bindings would allow. That voice…when it was masked with anger like that, she thought she recognized it from somewhere else…

"No, no." He hurried over to her side. "Don't be afraid of me. I'd never hurt you. Ever."

She cringed from him, and another look of fury crossed his face.

A cruel laugh left his lips. "Well, I suppose I did, once. Yes, I confess I took your virginity. It was mine to take, but I realize it must have hurt. That's all in the past, though. Now I'll love you and cherish you the way you deserve."

He smiled and she closed her eyes, before she jerked them open again in response to her cot moving.

However, it wasn't just the cot that moved but the entire floor.

She was on a boat.

Her captor chuckled. "That's right. They'll never find you here. We'll stay on the water forever. 'And they lived happily ever after.' That's what people will say about us in a few years."

CHAPTER TWENTY

NATE SAT IN THE SQUAD room rubbing his forehead. The police captain was busy handing out assignments. He knew he wouldn't be given an assignment because he wasn't part of the PD.

He'd promised Ryan he wouldn't do anything until they checked in at the station, pooling all of their resources, but to his knowledge, they knew nothing more than they'd known an hour ago.

His gut told him to go to the lake, but he didn't know why. If Ryan asked for a good reason, he couldn't give him one. His gut wasn't a good enough reason. He strolled over to the window facing the side of the building, wishing he could find some answers to his questions. The window was slightly open, letting in a nice breeze. Where did Trevor live? Where was Randy Brooks? Were they involved in her disappearance?

He heard a sound off to the side and turned his head, surprised to see a boy of about eight standing outside with a huge gray dog whose tongue was hanging out.

"Go to the loch." The boy nodded to him as if he were talking directly to him. All he could think of was what the hell did *that* mean? What was a "loch"? He turned to see if the lad was addressing someone behind him.

The boy chuckled. "Are ye daft, man? I said go to the loch."

He closed his eyes for a second, trying to gauge if the kid and the dog were really there, and when he opened them again, they were gone.

He rubbed his forehead again, looking for the boy, but he didn't see him or the dog. Could they have disappeared that quickly? Was he seeing things? Afraid his worry and concern for Lauren was clogging his mind, he turned back toward the officers' meeting.

Ryan came over and clapped a hand on his shoulder. "You see a ghost or something?"

Nate looked back at him with wide eyes. "Maybe. Or I could just be losing my mind. What's a loch?"

Ryan closed his eyes. "A loch is a lake. Why? Did you see something?" Something about the way he said it made Nate think he knew more about the situation than he was letting on. It emboldened him to speak.

"Did you see a boy or a dog there a moment ago? Is there one that lives down the street or something?"

Ryan quirked his brow. "Did he speak with an accent? Was it a huge deerhound or wolfhound or something?"

"Yeah," Nate said, suddenly relieved. "He said to go to the loch. Then he called me daft. Who uses the word daft in this day and age?"

"Old Scots," Ryan whispered. "I'll explain later. You and I are going to the lake. Don't mention the kid to anyone. I'll be right back."

Nate didn't know what to make of what Ryan Ramsay had said, but he didn't much care if Lauren's stepbrother had a screw loose. At least they were going to the lake.

Jake followed the two of them out to the cruiser. Ryan gave crisp instructions as they hurried along, as if he knew time was of the essence. "Jake, contact the sheriff's office, see if they'll send a boat out onto Orenda Lake."

"I don't know why you're going to the lake. There's no indication…"

Ryan stopped him in his tracks with one word. "Loki."

Jake's jaw dropped and his entire demeanor changed. "I'll make the arrangements. Get your ass going."

As soon as they were in the car, Nate asked, "What the hell did that mean? Who is Loki?"

Ryan put the car in gear and sped out of the parking lot. "You're not likely to believe this, and if I hadn't see it with my own eyes, I wouldn't believe it either, but Caitlyn was contacted by the boy and his pet a while ago, when she was in a bad state. He said he was her guiding angel."

"You mean guardian angel? Are you trying to tell me I just saw an angel?"

"Not guardian angel, guiding. He guides her in the right direction, which is exactly what he was doing with you. I told Jake about him."

Nate chuckled. "Come on, Ryan. You don't believe that, do you?"

"Like I said. If I hadn't seen him with my own eyes, I wouldn't believe it either. But I do trust my own eyes and ears."

"So what did he look like?"

"The dog is tall and thin. Gray haired with a wiry coat. The kid has brown hair, always mussed up, and he looks around eight or nine. Speaks with a Scottish burr, and comes off as the kind of jokester his name implies."

Nate took in everything Ryan said, unable to believe he'd talked with an apparition. "A ghost from Scotland. I don't know, Ramsay…What was he wearing?"

"His Grant plaid."

"What?"

"A kilt in muted reds and greens, a little gold. He's from medieval times, so the colors aren't really bright."

Nate whispered, "You saw him out the window."

Ryan said, "No, I didn't. If we find Lauren on the loch, I mean the lake, will you believe me then? Nothing gave us any reason to search the lake. It's September, and the temperature is only around fifty degrees. There won't be many boats out there now."

"Agreed. Tell me how you want to handle this. And who do you think we'll find?"

"Randy Brooks. His father and uncles all have boats and houses on the lake. He insisted someone would pay when we arrested the group at the frat house."

"Not Trevor?"

"Trevor is a little more mature than the others, but he's still a possibility." He pulled into the driveway, parked his cruiser, and both of them made a beeline to the lake. Ryan's father emerged from the house and followed them down.

"What is it, Three?"

"Dad, we're taking the boat. Lauren is missing. We have nothing to go on, just an inkling. I'll tell you as soon as we hear anything."

Lorraine had followed her husband out of the house. "Oh no," she said, reaching out to her husband. He wrapped his arms around her and helped hold her steady. "Please find her."

Ryan reached the boat-house and ducked in. A moment later, he came out with two vests—he put on one and tossed the other to Nate. "Use this in case bullets fly. If you go over, it'll keep you above water."

Nate didn't argue, he just put it on, struggling to get his numb hands to comply. He said a quick prayer, then thought of Lauren and what she must be going through.

He'd never met anyone as strong as Lauren. She had to hang on, she just had to. He'd started to imagine a future with her. With this woman he loved.

Once they headed out, Ryan pointed to the sheriff's boat already headed in their direction. Jake had been true to his word. Ryan slowed when the sheriff's boat drew up next to him. "Did you find anything?" he called out to the two guys on board.

"Ramsay, there's one boat out there," the man who was closer to them reported. "Plenty of room to hide someone. When we approached, we hadn't gotten your call yet, but I think it's worth checking out. He's trolling. Midway down on the east side of the lake. No fishing gear in sight."

"How many men?"

"Only saw one."

"Travel with us for backup?"

"Absolutely. Not much else happening out there this time of year. You make the call when we check it out. We'll follow your lead."

Ryan nodded and took off.

"You never asked him who it was," Nate said.

"Does it matter?"

Trevor Hutton removed Lauren's gag and ran his fingers down the side of her cheek. She backed away from him, coughing to get the awful sour taste out of her mouth. This wouldn't be the end. It couldn't be. Ryan and Jake would come for her, and Nate would search high and low for her.

But would they even consider checking the lake this late in the season?

"Water," she rasped.

Trevor moved over to the counter built into the side of the small room and grabbed a bottle of water. "Now, I'll leave that off if you can be pleasant and promise not to scream."

She nodded. As soon as she had reason to believe they were close to another boat or the shoreline, she'd scream her lungs out, but until that happened, she needed to convince him he could trust her.

She took several swigs of water, knowing she had to be dehydrated.

"I told Dominic not to hurt you. He was only supposed to scare you. In fact, I wish you'd never started that ridiculous support group. I sent Randy out to scare you, but I didn't tell him to set your house on fire. The stupid bastard. I beat the shit out of him for that mistake. You could have died. But you didn't listen to him or to the group. Your brothers wouldn't stop, and the school security was all over the fraternity. That's why it escalated. Dom and the others just like to play with a few women here and there. They never hurt them. None of them were virgins, and they all want it."

She didn't intend to argue with him. Ryan had told her to save her energy if she was ever abducted. Keep her strength up, be aware of her surroundings, and dig for information. Don't try to get away until there were others around, then scream and fight with all your strength.

Except she found herself saying, "He *did* hurt me. They all did, kicking and punching as if I were nothing but a rag doll."

His eyes glittered with rage and balled his fists. "I know, and I was furious when I saw that video. I'm glad Dom was arrested. I never intended for this. To see them touch you…hit you…it was just wrong. I apologize that I didn't get to you in time."

She said, "Where are we?"

"Orenda Lake." He moved over to a closet and opened it up. "Look at all the pretty things I bought for you." He pulled out one gown and said, "They're more weather appropriate for Florida, of course."

"Florida?" Her pulse sped up and she coughed again, doing her best to maneuver the water bottle with her hands tied in front of her.

He said, "My parents own two homes, one on the lake and one

in Florida. We'll occupy the one they're not in. They'll be leaving next week, so we'll have our own place until they return in late spring. By then, I expect you'll be used to the idea of being my wife."

"We're on the lake. You'll be caught if you try to bring me to Florida."

"Hardly. There's a small channel, as you know, that will take me into Seneca Lake. My parents own an old homestead there, too, though it's barely functional. No one will find us there. We'll set out once the search dies down."

"Trevor, you're a nice man," she said, trying to keep the tremor out of her voice as she addressed her rapist, "but I'm not interested in being your wife. A woman has to agree to the marriage, and I'll never marry you." She turned her head just a touch, not wanting him to see the disgust in her eyes. A distant sound registered in her ears. Was it truly a boat, or was she just projecting what she wanted to hear?

"Ah, but you will grow to love me. When you have no human contact but me, you'll become dependent on me. You'll see. You'll beg me to touch you in the end."

All of a sudden, he froze, tipping his head to the side.

"Shit," was all he said, but she knew that meant he'd heard the boat, too. She knew it was really there.

He grabbed her and hauled her around, holding her back against his belly. He pulled a gun out and said, "One word, one wrong movement, and I'll kill whoever it is. My guess is it's either that idiot boyfriend of yours or one of your stepbrothers. I'll kill all three of them if I need to."

CHAPTER TWENTY-ONE

"STAY OUT OF VIEW, NATE. I don't want him to know how many of us there are. Just stay hidden for now." Ryan slowed his engine as they approached the boat, the sheriff's vessel directly behind them. Their boat was a large fishing boat, so while there was no lower deck, the overhead area was large enough to protect the fishermen against the weather, which meant there was a wall for him to hide behind.

Nate took off his work boots and then the life vest.

"What the hell are you doing, Patterson?"

"I'm going in the water. If there's only one guy on board, you can keep him occupied, and I'll come up on the other side and take him by surprise. That's a good-sized boat. I have plenty of room to come up on the opposite side if you distract him. If I can't get to him, then I'll sneak below and see if I can find Lauren. I can't keep the life jacket on. I wouldn't be able to hide in the water."

"You realize the water is probably in the high fifties. You'll have to move fast."

"Adrenaline will carry me through. I love your stepsister."

Ryan gave him a small grin. "Can't argue with that reasoning. Be careful. We have to assume he's armed."

The sheriff pulled out his mic and said, "All occupants on deck, please."

Nate ducked behind the raised helm of the boat, giving himself a small area to watch the other boat. His worst fear materialized in front of him. Trevor Hutton emerged from the lower deck with Lauren in front of him, a gun aimed at the side of her head.

"You're going to leave now and let us go." Trevor appeared as calm as if he held a gun to someone's head on a regular basis. If Nate were to guess, he would not be easily distracted.

Nate didn't wait any longer. He shrugged out of his shirt and slid into the water on the far side of the boat. Damn it. Ramsay was right. The freaking water was cold. His nuts screamed at him to get out, but he persisted. After a few minutes, he'd adjusted enough to stop shivering, but he knew his time was limited. He moved to the far end of the boat and dropped underwater, swimming as fast as he could, careful not to let out any air bubbles to give himself away. He forced himself to swim far enough past Trevor's boat that he wouldn't be heard when he came up for air. When he finally did, he had to fight to keep from making any sound from the cold.

Fortunately, Ryan was distracting the kidnapper. "Not a chance, Hutton," he said, his voice carrying over the water. "Let go of Lauren, and I'll lift her into my boat."

"No. Your stepsister and I are getting married. I've always loved Lauren, but if I can't have her, no one will. If I die, I'm taking her with me. Her hands and feet are bound. I'll throw her over the side of the boat. She won't last long in this cold water."

"If you don't free her, we'll call for another ten boats to come and surround you. You'll run out of food, water, and gas. Don't make it come to that, Hutton."

Nate swam slowly over to the side of Trevor's boat, not stopping until he was directly behind him. He had a knife in his pants, but he had to get out of the water before he could unsheathe it. With any luck, he'd distract Trevor enough that the psycho would aim the gun at him instead of pulling the trigger on Lauren.

He made a quiet plea to all the guardian angels and guiding angels in the world to assist him with this attempt.

He just couldn't lose Lauren.

Trevor launched into another rant about the unjust world, so Nate decided it was time for him to make a grab for Lauren.

He threw himself over the side of the boat, and chaos ensued. Somehow he managed to yank out his dagger before Trevor turned around. He knocked Trevor's arm up in the air, hoping it would destroy his aim, and sunk his knife into his belly.

"Lauren, go below!" he shouted. He watched her struggle at the steps with her hands and feet bound, but all she managed to do was slide to the steps and sit on the edge. Fortunately, she could duck out of sight.

As soon as she was out of the way, gunfire burst from the two police boats. Nate was afraid to move, so he stayed put until Trevor dropped to the ground, at which point he swung his arms in the air to make sure they didn't keep shooting. He picked up the gun and hurried over to Lauren.

Desperate to have her in his arms, he dropped the gun to the floor and hugged her close, burying his face in her hair, her scent calming him, assuring him she was all right. He worked at her bindings while she babbled, "How did you know? I was so scared. He wanted to marry me and run away, and..."

"Hush, it's done. Finally done." His lips melded with hers, and he said a silent prayer of thanks to whoever had watched over them. Hell, he'd believe in ancient spirits and angels if they'd saved the love of his life. He pulled back and reached for her hands, finally untying the cords on her hands and feet. Lauren's sobs called to him, but the only thing that mattered to him was that she was free.

Finally free, or so he hoped.

When he had her hands out of the bindings, she wrapped her arms around his neck and sobbed into his shoulder, mumbling a volley of phrases, from which he made out "I love you," and "I was so scared."

He sat on the single cot below deck, taking her with him, and pulled back to inspect her for wounds. "You are all right? He didn't hurt you?"

"No," she said, gripping him tightly. "I'm fine. He's the one."

He was going to ask her "the one, what?" but Ryan appeared in the staircase. "Lauren, you're all right?"

"Yes. Ryan, he's the one."

Ryan stared at her in silence, waiting for her to finish.

"He's my rapist. He wanted to marry me, take me to Florida. As soon as his voice turned angry, I recognized him right away."

She leaned against Nate and said, "It's over. It's really over."

☾

Lauren discovered that it wasn't completely over, but at least the immediate threat on her person had ended.

With her help and the chart, Ryan and Jake were able to piece together a pattern in the attacks, and they finally discovered the other fraternity they suspected, Chi Theta had been responsible for many of the abuses.

The university shut down both frats and issued stern warnings to the remaining Greeks, both fraternities and sororities, about their purpose on campus.

The police chief met with several people at the university to rewrite the school's policy on suspected rape and abuse cases, making it mandatory to involve the outside police department. The security force on campus was not large enough to handle all the cases. New protocols were put in place to guide security on the handling of abuse cases, including how to contact family and how to deal with suspects and victims. Lauren was more than pleased with the progress the school made. She sent an email to the women in her group, explaining all that had happened and posting a date for their next meeting. After everything that had happened, she was eager to continue her work.

Lauren lay on the shore of the lake on the chaise lounge she'd pulled out of the boathouse an hour ago. In shorts and a tank top, she'd rushed down to enjoy what was bound to be one of the last warm days on Orenda Lake until spring. They'd been blessed with a warm day in mid-November, and she'd even skipped one of her graduate classes to wallow in the heat of the autumn sun. She'd cut a class. Never in her life had she cut a class, not even as an undergrad. The pull of the sun and the magical waters of the lake had won her over. She'd decided she was a new Lauren Grant, baptized by the horrors of what had happened on this lake. That meant taking risks and accepting—no, reveling in—her own lack of perfection. She'd even ducked her mother's request that she wear sunscreen.

She felt a bit naughty about that, especially since she still liked to mostly keep her mother happy, but it was a gorgeous autumn day in Western New York and she was unlikely to burn.

Closing her eyes, she tipped her head up to the sun, welcoming the warm rays across her body. The only thing that would make this moment more perfect was if Nate were beside her. These last months with him had been the best in her life. She'd never felt freer or more at peace.

She'd researched more about Alex Grant, though it had proven to be a difficult task. He'd been the laird of his clan, and they had a strong tie to Clan Ramsay, which had thrilled her to no end. Alex's sister had married the chieftain of the Ramsays, but everything she found out about them indicated they were dark-haired. She hadn't uncovered anything about Alex's wife, to her disappointment. Her mother and stepfather had been delighted to hear about her discovery.

A knocking sound interrupted her thoughts. She peeked out, but when she didn't see anything, she closed her eyes again and repositioned herself on the chair.

The knocking continued. She lifted her head again, closing one eye to see if she could keep the glare of the sun from interrupting her view of the water. Perhaps it was a stone banging against the dock or something like that.

Sighing, she leaned back, but the noise became even more obnoxiously loud, so she finally sat up and glanced around. Yep, she was definitely alone, and the sound was definitely coming from the water. Giving up, she got out of her chair, slipped into her flip-flops, and moved down to the water.

She padded across the dock, but there didn't appear to be anything in the water, though the noise hadn't abated. When she reached the end, she determined she was farther away from the sound than before, so she spun around and headed back toward shore, finally locating the sound when she reached the rocks by the dock. Something sat in the lake, knocking against the rocks with each lap of the water against the shoreline.

Shrugging, she headed back to her lounge chair, only to stop and turn around to stare at the object. Curiosity finally propelled her back to the shore. It was a glass bottle with the label missing. She bent over to retrieve it, telling herself it was the right thing to do, when something caught her eye up close.

A rolled piece of paper sat inside the bottle. It was probably something a ten-year old boy had sent across the lake. Spencer had done the same thing several times. She opened the bottle and pulled out the rolled-up scroll. Dropping the bottle onto the grass for a moment, she opened the paper and read:

I'm not very good with words, but I think you know that by now. Here goes: I love you and I want us to be together forever. Lauren Grant, will you make me the happiest man alive and marry me? Love, Nate

She squealed and twirled around, looking for Nate. How could she have missed him? He stepped out of the boat-house and said, "Well?"

She took off on a dead run toward him, launching herself into his arms with a screech, saying, "Yes, yes, yes, Nate Patterson." She kissed him and said, "I love you more than I thought was possible. Thank you for showing me what love is supposed to be."

She kissed him again, sighing with satisfaction as he teased her with his tongue. When he ended the kiss, he said, "I love you, and I promise to cherish you forever, but it took you long enough to get out of that chair to find the bottle. I was on pins and needles out here."

She threw her head back with a laugh. "The sun is so warm. I was thinking of you when I was lying there. Where did you put it in the water? How did you know it would come to me? Oh, and where did you park? I didn't see your truck."

He took her hand and headed to the shoreline. "I had a little help from someone I met before. I didn't know who he was at the time, but he's the one who told me to look for you in the lake when you were missing."

He had his arm around her, rubbing his hand up and down her hip. "Loki, where are you?" he asked.

Lauren stared at him, wide-eyed. "Loki? What kind of name is that?"

"Norse, though he's Gaelic. Oh, never mind. Loki? Don't make me look like a fool."

Out of nowhere, two objects landed in the water at the end of the dock. A moment later, a dog's head popped out of the water, and the dog, a Scottish deerhound, paddled toward shore. A second head, that of a young boy, popped up next to him. He raced out of the water with a loud yelp. "Och, 'tis almost as cold as the Scottish lochs Papa used to make me bathe in. Come on, Growley. We have a few minutes."

Lauren whispered, "Who is that? Where did he come from?" She clutched Nate's arm.

"Lauren, meet Loki and his dog Growley. They know Ryan and Caitlyn. Tell her where you're from, Loki."

"Aye, we're from Scotland. Growley and I travel whenever

we're needed. I prefer to come as a ten-year-old. But I could have turned eleven waiting for you to pick up that bottle." Loki glanced up above toward the sky, "Aye, Papa. I recall my manners." He moved over to stand in front of Lauren, then bowed to her and said, "Greetings to you from the Scots. I'm from the Highlands. The year 1263 was my favorite. That one and then twenty years later in the 1280s with my sweet Bella. I'm glad you went back for the bottle. I was tiring of hiding under the dock and pushing it your way. Aunt Maddie and Uncle Alex made me promise to help you."

He spun around, but then pivoted back to say, "Watch this." He charged down the dock and jumped off the end as high as he could, gathering his legs tight to make a large splash.

Lauren was right behind him. She could swear the lad had said 1263, and something else caught her attention. "Don't go, please don't go. Not yet." She said a quick prayer to God and any angel who would listen to her. "Please, please send him back. I couldn't understand everything he said."

Loki's head popped up, sputtering and laughing. "Was that not a big one? I haven't left yet. You need not pray."

He swam to the ladder and started to climb out, but Lauren loomed over him, tears in her eyes. "Did you say 1263? Do you know anything about the Battle of Largs? Uncle Alex and Aunt who?"

Loki climbed up the ladder, squirming around her. "Aye, I fought in the Battle of Largs. Did you not know that? Does it not say in your history books that the Scottish warriors used slingers?" He ran to the start of the dock and grabbed a couple of small stones from the shore, producing something from his pocket that he held up, demonstrating how far he could fling the rocks. "I felled a few of my own Norsemen. But Uncle Alex was the best. He had his golden helm on. He swung his sword like this," he shouted, imitating a warrior battling.

He quit his play suddenly and started toward the end of the dock. "'Course Papa was also a fearsome presence in that battle. Come on, Growley." The large deerhound got up from his spot in the lawn, lumbering behind Loki down the dock. "We must go before we're discovered."

"Wait, please!" Lauren shouted. If she could only talk to him for half an hour.

"One more question, my lady." The lad stopped halfway down the dock to turn to her, waiting for her question.

Lauren had at least a thousand. "Alex Grant's wife. What does she look like?" Tears poured down her cheeks. "Please?"

"Aunt Maddie? Aye, she's got yellow hair and a heart of gold and a mark right here near her eye." He pointed to his right eye. "Uncle Alex loves her. We all do. She's verra special. She's your ancestor. We're all related from many moons ago."

Loki yelled, "Watch this one!" With one more leap, he landed in the water and disappeared, Growley behind him.

"Nate, is he a ghost or something? He didn't die in the water, did he?"

"No. that's what he does. He appears out of nowhere and then disappears. He did the same with Cait and Ryan. She saw him when she was in an accident. What's wrong?"

Tears flooded her cheeks. "I'm not crazy. I saw this woman when I fell asleep. Twice. She told me that you're my Alex...Alex Grant was who she meant. I thought I was losing my mind at first. I thought...but her hair was blonde and she had a mole right where he said." Her finger reached up to rub the spot, still unable to believe that she'd actually communicated with someone from medieval times. How was it possible?

Nate kissed her, stopping her from communicating her worst fears out loud. "There's nothing wrong with you, Lauren Grant. Have I told you what my middle name is?"

"No. What is it?"

"Alexander. I was christened Nathan Alexander Patterson."

"Oh, Nate. You are my Alex."

She rubbed her thumb across his bottom lip as she repeated Maddie's words. "Forever honorable. Always trustworthy. And a most gentle and loving man. I love you."

EPILOGUE

LAUREN WAS ESPECIALLY NERVOUS TODAY, though she did her best to hide it. After all the times she'd hidden her true feelings from her family over the last few years, this should be easy.

Nate leaned over her shoulder to pick up the serving bowl of tossed salad he was about to carry onto the porch at the lake house. "You'll be great, love."

She sighed and smiled at him.

Thanksgiving Day had come so quickly, it had almost taken her by surprise. Her nightmares had receded so much that she was down to maybe one or two a month. Spending time in Nate's protective arms had helped her to take control of her PTSD from her attacks. Yes, she knew she'd probably have them forever, but it was as her stepbrother had said—they no longer controlled her.

The door came open with a huff and there was a flurry of foot stomps to get rid of the dusting of snow outside. Sam and Tristan stood inside the door removing their coats and then handed Lorraine a bouquet of flowers and a bottle of wine.

Nate whistled. "Wow, I'm impressed. Two gifts. Well done, Sam."

Tristan's voice came out in a slight bellow. "Hey. The wine was my idea. That's what my date last week said to bring."

"Would she like to come?" Lauren asked. "You know we always have room for more."

"No..." Tristan stuttered.

Sam chuckled, "Tristan can get dates, he just hasn't figured out how to get a second one." Tristan scowled, then stalked away from his brother to join the group in front of the football game.

Ryan Sr. came out of the kitchen with the turkey just then, setting it into the middle of the table, and they all helped carry out the rest of the feast. The porch was their largest room, so they dined there whenever the entire family was present. With three tables for all the guests, it took them a while for everyone to find their place, but once grace was finished, the large group of Grants and Ramsays and extras dug into the food with expressions of joy and anticipation.

"This looks wonderful, Lorraine," Julia said.

Jake added, "Smells great, too."

Mallory said, "I can't wait to eat."

It wasn't long until the group quieted as everyone began to tuck into their food.

"Oh my," Julia said.

Lauren knew exactly what she meant. Everyone followed her gaze to Tristan's plate heaped with turkey, mashed potatoes, and stuffing.

The pleasant chiding began:

"What, no vegetables, Tristan?"

"Can you really eat all that?"

"I've never seen anyone eat that many mashed potatoes."

"He'll eat more…"

"No way!"

Tristan continued to eat, ignoring them all. The expression on his face told them all he was in his glory, enjoying every bite, and that he wouldn't allow anyone to interfere with the pleasure he was taking in the food on his plate.

Once they finished, Tristan pushed back from the table with a smile. "That was great, Lorraine."

"Would you like more?"

He shook his head.

The chorus immediately piped up:

"Have some more, Tristan."

"He can't eat any more."

"I can't believe he ate two platefuls."

"He did eat something green on the second plate."

"Won't he get sick from eating that much?"

They all laughed and teased Tristan, but he didn't seem to mind. If anything, he seemed to enjoy being the center of attention.

Lauren finally stood up and waited for everyone to quiet down. "I have so much to be thankful for this year. Your assistance and support are so appreciated. I've never been happier than I am now. I wanted to share some news that Nate and I have..."

Lorraine gasped and brought her napkin up to her mouth, her eyes misting.

Lauren pulled Nate up to stand next to her and she gazed into his eyes as she made their announcement. "Nate has asked me to marry him and I have accepted." She pulled the ring from her pocket where she'd hidden it, sliding it onto her finger so all could see it. He'd chosen a beautiful setting, a round halo setting in white gold.

Cait squealed and jumped out of her chair, pulling Ryan with her. "I'm so excited! You two are wonderful together."

The group broke into applause and cheers, everyone getting up out of their seats to congratulate the couple. When they finally settled back into their places, a quiet voice interrupted them.

Tristan said, "Congratulations to you, but would someone mind passing the potatoes?"

They all turned to stare at him in unison.

"What? I think I can fit a few more."

THE END

NOVELS BY KEIRA MONTCLAIR

THE CLAN GRANT SERIES

#1- RESCUED BY A HIGHLANDER-Alex and Maddie
#2- HEALING A HIGHLANDER'S HEART-
Brenna and Quade
#3- LOVE LETTERS FROM LARGS-Brodie and Celestina
#4-JOURNEY TO THE HIGHLANDS-Robbie and Caralyn
#5-HIGHLAND SPARKS-Logan and Gwyneth
#6-MY DESPERATE HIGHLANDER-Micheil and Diana
#7-THE BRIGHTEST STAR IN THE HIGHLANDS-
Jennie and Aedan
#8- HIGHLAND HARMONY-Avelina and Drew

THE HIGHLAND CLAN

LOKI-Book One
TORRIAN-Book Two
LILY-Book Three
JAKE-Book Four
ASHLYN-Book Five
MOLLY-Book Six
JAMIE AND GRACIE- Book Seven
SORCHA-Book Eight
KYLA-Book Nine
BETHIA-Book Ten
LOKI'S CHRISTMAS STORY-Book Eleven

THE SOULMATE CHRONICLES

#1 TRUSTING A HIGHLANDER

THE SUMMERHILL SERIES- CONTEMPORARY ROMANCE

#1-ONE SUMMERHILL DAY

#2-A FRESH START FOR TWO

#3-THREE REASONS TO LOVE

REGENCY

THE DUKE AND THE DRESSMAKER

DEAR READERS,

Thank you for reading *Three Reasons to Love*. If you haven't read my historical novels, you'll find some of the angel characters there. Maddie was first introduced in *Rescued by a Highlander* and Loki appeared first in *Love Letters from Largs*. They have both been in many of the historical novels in both series: Clan Grant and The Highland Clan.

I have no immediate plans for the next Summerhill novel, so you may not see another until 2019. Instead, I'm planning the first in a new historical series. I can't wait for you to read it!

Until then, I hope you'll try one of my historical novels. There are many to choose from, and they are wonderful family sagas.

Happy reading!

Keira Montclair

www.keiramontclair.com
www.facebook.com/KeiraMontclair
www.pinterest.com/KeiraMontclair

ABOUT THE AUTHOR

Keira Montclair is the pen name of an author who lives in Florida with her husband. She loves to write fast-paced, emotional romance, especially with children as secondary characters in her stories.

She has worked as a registered nurse in pediatrics and recovery room nursing. Teaching is another of her loves, and she has taught both high school mathematics and practical nursing.

Now she loves to spend her time writing, but there isn't enough time to write everything she wants! Her Highlander Clan Grant series, comprising of eight standalone novels, is a reader favorite. Her third series, The Highland Clan, set twenty years after the Clan Grant series, focuses on the Grant/Ramsay descendants. She also has a contemporary series set in The Finger Lakes of Western New York.

Her newest series is The Soulmate Chronicles, historical romance with a touch of paranormal.

Made in the USA
San Bernardino, CA
11 February 2018